Readers love
GENE GANT

In Time I Dream About You

"It is gritty, unflinchingly honest, and yet allows for the dream of a better life to be realized in the end. It is an excellent novel that I recommend to you."

—The Novel Approach

"…this is an excellent read… the combination of social issues and futuristic escapism is a great combination that makes this story worth a read."

—Joyfully Jay

Bender

"I do like the author's style of storytelling, and can't wait for more from him."

—Oh My Shelves

Lucky Linus

"Linus is lucky to finally be granted his wish and readers will be lucky to be on a journey with him."

—Paddylast Inc.

"This book totes a wide range of variety, creating an important voice for an overlooked, small clique of trivialized teens."

—Great Imaginations

By GENE GANT

Published by HARMONY INK PRESS
www.harmonyinkpress.com

GENE GANT

King Geordi the Great

Harmony Ink

Published by

HARMONY INK PRESS

5032 Capital Circle SW, Suite 2, PMB# 279, Tallahassee, FL 32305-7886 USA
publisher@harmonyinkpress.com • harmonyinkpress.com

King Geordi the Great
© 2018 Gene Gant.

Cover Art
© 2018 Kanaxa.
Cover content is for illustrative purposes only and any person depicted on the cover is a model.

ISBN: 978-1-64080-092-2
Digital ISBN: 978-1-64080-093-9
Library of Congress Control Number: 2017911058
Published January 2018
v. 1.0

Printed in the United States of America

This paper meets the requirements of
ANSI/NISO Z39.48-1992 (Permanence of Paper).

CHAPTER 1

DADS. YOU'LL find plenty of variation on that theme.

There's Workaholic Dad, for example. He lives, breathes, boozes, woos, and screws his job, twenty-four seven. You often wonder how you and your mom ever factored into his life equation. He's not there for the first day of kindergarten, the school play, the dance recital, the football game, bar mitzvah, quinceañera, graduation, or any other significant event in your life. Broke an arm and want your dad there with you in the emergency room? Sorry, the boss called with a special project and a deadline of yesterday. Boyfriend dumped you and you need to cry on your dad's shoulder? Tough, he's out of town for a three-week sales conference and can't take your blubbering phone call.

There's Indifferent Dad. He's around and available when you need him, but the thing is he just doesn't give a shit. He couldn't care less that you made honor roll *and* the basketball team. Don't think for one second he's ever going to pat you on the back and say how proud you've made him. No, he won't do that even when the mayor gives you a citation for meritorious service after you organize a car wash that raises almost a thousand dollars for the city's homeless shelter. Hell no, Indifferent Dad just wants you to leave him alone.

There's Strict Dad. He's all about the straight and narrow. Veer off that path and he comes down on you like Batman on the Joker. Flunked a history exam? BAM! You're grounded for a week. Complain to Strict Dad that you studied hard and being grounded a whole week is unfair? POW! You're grounded for two. Open your mouth again and it's straight to Arkham Asylum. *If* you're lucky.

There's Alcoholic Dad, perhaps the saddest of them all. When he drinks too much, which is far too often, he gets into loud, horrible fights with your mom that snatch all the joy out of the house. Ugh. Let's not linger on this one.

Of course, there's Good Ol' Dad, also known as the Andy Griffith/ Ward Cleaver Dad, beamed straight out of the 1950s. He works hard, yes, but mostly to ensure you have all that you need and everything you ever want. But no matter how hard he works, he always has time for you. Got a crush on a girl and don't have a clue how to ask her out? Call Good Ol' Dad at the office. He'll put his all-important client on hold to dole out some quick pointers. Want him to take you bowling on Saturday? No problem, he's right there, and you'll even get pizza afterward. Need some cash for an afternoon at the movies with your friends? Good Ol' Dad is your personal ATM.

Then there's *my* dad.

God help me.

My dad's in a category all his own.

LET ME say this up front. My dad loves me. Totally and unconditionally. No matter where I go, no matter what I do or don't do, I know he's got my back. Always.

Now my mom loves me too, of course. She's there to pick me up and cheer me on when I need it. She's a great parent. Dad, on the other hand, is an überparent. His heart's as good as a box of Skittles, but his brain comes straight out of a Terminator. His mind has no filter and recognizes no boundaries.

Here's an example of what I mean. Like a lot of kids, I didn't really think much about nakedness and bathroom stuff when I was small. A baby can't change a diaper on its own, and a toddler left alone in a bathtub is more likely to flood the room (or drown) than get himself clean. So your parents take care of those things for you, and it's no big deal that they routinely see you in your birthday suit. Naturally, as I grew, I gradually took on the responsibility for my personal hygiene until my folks were out of the loop completely. By my eleventh birthday, I was paranoid about my body and didn't want anyone to even see me in my underwear, let alone naked.

Mom got it. She always knocked and asked if I was decent before coming into my room. Once when I accidentally dropped my bath towel in the toilet bowl after climbing out of the tub, Mom kept her head turned when she handed me a replacement through the door. When she took me shopping for clothes, she stayed clear of the dressing room while I tried on different pairs of pants. Yay Mom!

Dad never got it. He threw a big bash for me when I turned twelve. Because my birthday is in June and my parents had just installed a gorgeous new in-ground pool, he decided to make it a pool party. Twenty-six kids showed up, including a bunch I knew from school. The festivities started at five that evening. The temperature hit the predicted high of one hundred degrees by midafternoon, and my parents didn't want the fun spoiled by an inconvenient case of atomic sunburn or creeping heat stroke. Everything was great for about two and a half hours until the sun went down and night came on. The party started winding down, and with everyone out of the pool, I decided to show off a bit before my guests got away. I climbed up on the diving board and did a forward somersault with a twist. It was a dive Dad had taught me. Applause and shouts erupted while I was in the air, so I knew I'd nailed it. Oh yeah, I was absolutely badass!

Until I hit the water. My trunks were oversized, which was the way all the guys I knew wore them. Somehow the force of the plunge ripped the trunks right off me, and suddenly I was skinny-dipping. Fortunately no one else was in the water, and neither the pool nor patio lights were on yet. Unfortunately my wayward trunks went on a deep-sea dive, and it was too dim for me to see the bottom of the pool.

Dad was standing by the diving board, watching for me to come up. After a quick, frantic, futile search for my swimwear, I surfaced and swam over to him, my face burning with embarrassment.

"Great dive, Geordi!" Dad said, grinning at me. "You hit the water perfectly."

I didn't have time for his compliments. Covering my private parts with one hand while treading water with the other, I whispered, "I lost my trunks, Dad. They're in the pool somewhere. It's kinda dark... I can't see them."

His face twitched a bit but the grin never wavered. "Oh. Okay. Hang on."

Dad headed for the house. I figured he was going to get another pair of trunks, which he would subtly pass to me, and I would discreetly slip into, thus sparing myself death by utter embarrassment. Unfortunately, several friends were hurrying my way, whooping about the dive. Once they got close enough, they'd see a lot more of me than anybody wanted, especially yours truly. I sucked in a deep breath, went under, and swam as fast as I could for the opposite end of the pool. With distance, the shadows apparently hid me well enough that no one could tell the direction of my swim. When I surfaced at the end of the pool, no one else was there. Fantastic. A huge shrub grew just a few feet away. I thought that, under cover of deepening darkness, I'd be able to climb out of the pool and duck behind the shrub before anyone saw me.

I hauled myself out of the water and made a dash for the shrub. After I took two steps, the lights went on in the pool and over the patio, along with the landscaping lights scattered across the backyard. The whole place blazed bright as day. There were my trunks, drifting lazily through the deep water below the diving board. There was my dad—and all my party guests—standing just a pool's length away. And there I was, frozen in place with my little jewels and my skinny butt lit up for all to see.

For a moment all the kids at the other end of the pool were frozen too. Then the hoots and howls started, and the cell phones came out, camera lenses aimed at me with YouTube only a thumb tap away, and I jumped behind the shrub as if my life depended on it. About a minute later, I heard Dad call out to me.

"Okay, Geordi. Now that I've got the lights on, I see your trunks right here, just a few feet from the diving board. Come get 'em."

A merciful God would have let me die behind that bush.

After the party I thought my name had changed to Saw-You-Naked.

The next day, for instance, I was taking a shortcut through the park when I ran into the Baxter triplets, Trina, Rina, and Ina. (If you're thinking their parents should be arrested for that, I'm with you 100 percent.) Here's how that went:

Me (my face feeling as red as a stop sign): "Uh… hey Trina, Rina, and Ina."

Trina (smiling wickedly): "Saw…."

Rina (ditto on the mean smile): "…you…."

Ina (evil grin in triplicate): "…naked!"

Then all three of them giggled as they walked away.

And later that day, when I was headed to the movies with Toff—who is my best friend and would never laugh at me, at least not in such a bad way—I ran into Carson Meyer. Carson had a rep as the best basketball player in the neighborhood, until yours truly started playing the game. That began a longstanding, not exactly friendly rivalry between us, and Carson was always looking for some way to one-up me both on court and off. Here's how the day-after encounter with him went:

Me (not so embarrassed because Carson's a guy, and surely a guy wouldn't make a big deal out of seeing another guy naked): "Hey, Carson. What's up?"

Carson (nasty grin borrowed from the Baxter sisters): "Saw you naked when you got out of the pool. That water must've been *hella* cold." To drive the point home, Carson went for overkill and held his hand up in front of my face with the tips of his thumb and index finger about a half inch apart. I was a wee bit small down there, sure. But a half inch? *Really?*

This was way worse than the Baxter trips. A couple of kids I didn't even know pointed at me and burst out laughing. Three-pointer for Carson. Dag! It was literally and figuratively a low blow. I mean, what do you expect a twelve-year-old guy to have down there? I couldn't even think up a comeback to blast on Carson. The only thing I could do was slink into the theater with my head down and hope the whole saw-you-naked thing would blow over soon.

It went on for a whole, entire, miserable, and very long week.

All thanks to my dad.

Oh, but there was worse to come. A couple of months later, on a quiet Saturday morning at home, I was shut away in the bathroom at the end of the hall. It was the bathroom I always used because it was the one closest to my room. Football season was starting, and Dad had gone out to the store to pick up some new gear for us to wear to the first game. I heard the garage door go up when he returned, followed by the sound of his footsteps moving through the kitchen. "Where's Geordi?" he asked.

"I think he's in the bathroom," Mom replied.

Dad's footsteps sounded in the hall, quickly coming my way. I got the impression he had something urgent to tell me. Now a normal father, confronted with a closed bathroom door, would have just knocked and delivered his message through the door, or waited until his kid emerged. Dad's mind didn't work that way. Instead of doing the reasonable, courteous thing, he shoved the bathroom door open and barged right in.

"Listen, Geordi, I went to five stores and couldn't find those Titans caps we wanted. I did find a Cowboys cap and a Bengals cap. We both like those teams, so I thought you could pick one and I'll take the other. How's that sound?" He held the two caps out in front of me.

I glared at him so hard it felt as if my eyeballs had turned to rock.

He blinked at me. "What's eating you?"

"Dad, I am sitting on the toilet."

"Oh, that's okay. Go ahead and finish your business. What do you think about getting jerseys to match the caps?"

Sschhrrriiippp!

That was the sound of me tearing out my hair.

But wait! Believe it or not, it got *even worse*.

A couple of months before I turned thirteen, puberty hit me with both barrels. My voice started squeaking, my clothes stopped fitting, hair sprouted in the weirdest places, and my nipples got tender and lumpy. To this day I freak out when I remember that last one. I thought it meant I was going to need bras. On the plus side, my junk got bigger. *Yes!*

The downside to the plus side was that my penis also developed a mind of its own. It would get hard without any provocation, and at the oddest damn moments. Like when I was standing in the serving line at the school cafeteria and the lady with the hairnet behind the counter dished up my favorite food, tater tots. Or when I was helping the mother of a very close friend unload groceries from her car. For a while there, I worried I had a thing for middle-aged women. I mean, how sexy is flinging tater tots?

With all that swelling testosterone, I quickly discovered the joy of jacking off. I jacked off a lot. You'd have thought I was in a masturbating marathon. I did it in the morning when I woke up, in the afternoon when I got home from school, before dinner, after dinner, just about every chance I got. A few weeks after my thirteenth birthday, I was home alone on a late Thursday afternoon while my parents were next door oohing and ahhing over the neighbors' new baby. It was a perfect opportunity for me to do a little gland-handling. I went into my room and closed the door—but didn't lock it as I usually did when my parents were in the house. After that bathroom conference with my dad over NFL caps last autumn, I'd started locking doors when I wanted privacy. I was so eager to get hands-on with myself, however, I didn't even want to lose the extra seconds it would take to turn the lock. Which should have been no big deal since my parents weren't home.

So there I was lying on my bed, my jeans and tighty-whities shoved down to my knees, staring at one of my favorite provocative movie sequences on my TV screen while I worked away in an ever-increasing frenzy. Things were getting really heated, the intensity building by the second, my face scrunching with passion. The magic moment was getting closer... closer... and then—

Dad waltzed in.

"Geordi, have you seen my cell phone? I can't—"

"*Aaarrrrhhhh!*"

That was me, screaming like a girl. (Seriously, how long does it take a voice to change?)

I snatched the pillow from behind my head, used it to cover my shriveling private parts, threw myself off the bed, and took cover in the closet. "Dad, get out! Get out, get out, *get out!*"

"What's all the fuss about, Geordi? I've seen your penis before. And you're thirteen. You're just doing what thirteen-year-old guys do. It's not like your mom and I don't know, son." And then he laughed.

Yes, you read that right. He *laughed.* I was in the closet burning up with shame, so humiliated I didn't think I'd ever walk in daylight again, but my invasion-force dad was having himself a good ol' time.

"God, Dad, just get out!" I yelled for something like a minute, but Dad didn't budge. I could sense the man was still standing there. Then I noticed something odd. He wasn't saying anything, and that was highly unusual for him. Dad *always* had something to say. So I stopped yelling, opened the closet door, and peeked out to see what he was up to.

He was staring at my TV screen, and he wasn't smiling anymore. In fact, the expression on his face was sort of stunned. Then, with my heart sinking like a torpedoed battleship, I realized what he was looking at.

There was a movie I kept in my Netflix queue, *Nurse 3D*. I didn't know anything about the movie's plot because I'd never watched the whole thing. I just knew that Corbin Bleu was in it. Corbin Bleu was an actor who featured very prominently in many of my fantasies and wet dreams. I'd fast forwarded and paused the movie on a scene where Corbin was naked and having sex with a woman, presumably the titular nurse. You could see the actress's legs and high-heeled feet, but if you were interested in naked lady parts—and I wasn't, not one bit—nothing of the kind was on display. The emphasis of the shot was clearly on Corbin's body. His paused-in-action, very round, very smooth, very fine, very masculine butt filled the screen.

Dad turned from that image, looked right at me, and gasped, "Geordi. Are you gay?"

Looking back, I realize now this was more than just another turning point in my family's history. It was the moment my dad went from merely driving me crazy to actively destroying my life.

SEVERAL SECONDS passed with the two of us just staring at each other. Dad seemed tense, but I couldn't tell exactly what he was feeling, and I started getting afraid.

Then he turned away. "Pull up your pants and come with me," he said as he walked out of my room.

Fastening the jeans at my waist, I followed him up the hall to the living room, where he pointed me to the sofa. Just as I sat down, Mom returned from visiting the neighbors, humming happily as she let herself in through the front door. She looked at me and smiled. Then she looked at Dad, and her humming fizzled to silence.

"Diana, I have to tell you something," Dad said, his voice as severe as the expression on his face.

"What is it?" Mom said apprehensively, her eyes shifting back and forth between Dad and me.

"You'd better sit down for this."

"Ben, you're scaring me."

"Please, Diana."

Dad took Mom's hand and led her to the sofa. She sat on one side of me and Dad sat on the other.

"Now what is this about?" Mom snapped, anxiety making her hands twitch.

"I just saw Geordi whacking off in his room."

Mom collapsed against the backrest of the sofa as if all the bones had been sucked out of her body. A grin of relief swept across her face. "Geordi's playing with himself. Oh, come on, Ben. That sure as hell isn't news to anybody." She looked at me and chuckled heartily.

I was really getting tired of being laughed at.

"It's not the whacking off per se you need to know about," Dad said, still looking solemn. "It's what he was whacking off to."

The worry came back to Mom's face. She flicked her eyes at me and looked at Dad again. "What do you mean?"

Dad took a deep breath. "He was masturbating while looking at a movie scene of some naked, curly-headed guy's butt."

Mom put a hand to her mouth. Her eyes got wide. I think she stopped breathing for a moment. Then she drew in her own deep breath, looked at me again, exhaled, and asked, "Geordi, are you gay?"

I didn't answer when Dad asked me that question earlier. I didn't want to answer it now. For weeks I'd been fantasizing about guys, looking at pictures of their bare bodies, and getting super excited, but I'd never really thought about what that meant. It was just something new I'd discovered about myself, and it felt natural to me. Gay was a concept I understood well enough. I'd simply never considered whether it applied to me.

But here were my parents now, looking… disturbed. And they were asking me a question to which, I suddenly realized, we all knew the answer. Because straight guys don't jack off while looking at pictures of naked men. They just don't.

That's when the fear came fully down on me. I'd read stories on the internet about teen homelessness. Many homeless teens were on the street because they were gay, lesbian, bi, trans—something other than hetero—and their parents, for some awful reason, couldn't deal with it. Their parents threw them away without a second thought.

I didn't want my parents to throw me away.

Mom was giving me this really intense look. She leaned toward me, and I could see her body trembling, could hear how rapidly she was breathing. "It's true, isn't it?"

I started hyperventilating myself. Dad was staring at me too, and I feared what was surely to come from my parents: outrage, disgust, bitter tears, blistering curses. Neither of them had ever laid a hand on me in anger before, but maybe that was about to change. I cringed between them, shaking in terror, waiting for their wrath to thunder down on me.

"Oh my God. It *is* true." Mom's entire face suddenly lit up with joy, and she wrapped her arms around my neck, pulling me to her in a hug so tight it made my eyes bug out. "My sweet baby boy is gay!"

Behind me, I could hear Dad doing that crazed whooping he unleashed at football games when his team scored. "Way to go, son! Whoo-hoo!" And then he started clapping me on the shoulder with gusto.

I exploded into loud, gasping, ugly-face sobs.

"Oooh, oooh," Mom cooed at me, rubbing my back with her hands. "What's the matter, Geordi hon? Why are you crying?"

"I'm so confused!" I wailed.

"Confused about what?" Dad asked.

"I thought you were mad at me for being gay. I thought you were gonna hate me and kick me out."

Mom pushed away from me so she could look into my eyes. "Mad at you? Hate you? Oh honey…." She wiped away my tears with her thumbs, the most loving smile glowing on her face. "Your dad and I would never hate you or be angry with you for who you are. We love you no matter what."

"Of course we do," Dad added, slipping his arm around my shoulders and hugging me. "Your mom and I… well, we sort of suspected you were gay, and it's just so wonderful to finally have it out in the open. This is not something for you to be ashamed of, son, not in the least. We've always been proud of you, and nothing has changed that. So stop that silly crying. This is cause for celebration!"

I felt better right away, touched especially by my dad's words. I didn't really expect any kind of actual celebration, however. He was just speaking rhetorically or whatever when he said that, and I knew it.

Yeah. Right.

Stupid me.

CHAPTER 2

OKAY, FAST-FORWARD a couple of years.

It was July, and my lazy summer days were spent mostly with Toff and my other best friend in the world, Jessica Sanchez. For the record, Jessica's heritage is Mexican, my bloodline is African, and Toff is persuasion Caucasian. Mom said the three of us were diversity in action.

Toff's legal name, by the way, is Sandor Regis Toffler, after his mom's dad. Kids kept calling him Sandy because Sandor sounds sort of snooty (or at least I thought so), and he *hated* being Sandy. "What am I? A beach?" he complained the first time I called him that. His attitude got me angry enough to want him out of my house, and I retorted with "So take off, then!" Only it came out sounding like, "So t'off, then!" He thought it was a nickname clipped from Toffler, he actually liked it, and he's had everybody calling him Toff ever since. I envied him, being named after his grandfather, and I would have been proud to be called Sandor, or even Sandy, if I were him. My name is Geordi La Forge Quintrell. My dad was such a big fan of *Star Trek: The Next Generation*, he named me after his favorite character on the show. I suppose I should be thankful his favorite character wasn't Worf.

Anyway, Jessica and Toff showed up at my house the Saturday after Independence Day. It was completely unexpected, because we usually texted before dropping in on each other.

"What're you guys doing here?" I asked, happy to see them in any event.

"We three are going to the movies," Jessica said.

That was news to me. The three of us OD'd on movies during the summer, making it a point to catch every single action, sci-fi, comedy, animated, horror, and superhero blockbuster the studios shoveled at the public. So far, we'd seen eight flicks with seven more still to come on our to-do list, but none of those were scheduled for release this weekend.

"To watch what?" I was already pulling on my sneakers, which shows how little I cared about the answer.

"I wanna see that new Godzilla movie again," Toff replied.

"Cool with me." I'd spent all my allowance yesterday on graphic novels. Luckily Mom had given me twenty bucks out of the blue at breakfast this morning. She called it an advance on next week's allowance, something she'd never done before, but I wasn't about to question her on it. I grabbed the unexpected cash off my dresser and stuffed it in my pocket. "Let's go."

At fifteen—well, fourteen for Jessica—none of us were licensed to drive, so we set out on foot for the twenty-minute walk to our favorite multiplex. We started out chatting happily with each other, but about fifteen minutes later, we sort of lapsed into silence. That wasn't because we ran out of topics of conversation; we ran out of breath.

"Whew!" Jessica gasped. "Could it be any hotter?" The pink midlength tank top and cutoff blue jeans she wore left her arms, shoulders, and legs bare. Her light brown skin appeared to be getting browner by the second. She was willowy at six feet, taller than either Toff or me, but one day soon, we were finally going to start gaining on her—I hoped. Because of her height, the rumor going around school this past year was that she was a total lez. I felt bad about that, because she was really pretty and as feminine as any other girl I knew, but she didn't seem to be all that bothered by the allegation.

"It's barely noon, and it already feels like the temp has hit a hundred degrees." Toff lifted the front of his T-shirt and wiped sweat from his face. He had wild glossy brown hair that he kept trimmed short in the summer. His body was lean and athletic, sort of like mine but in a better way, and he had a face that was cute by any standards despite being dotted here and there with tiny red pimples and occasionally weighed down by a hangdog expression. (My face is cuter, in my humble and completely unbiased opinion.)

"We don't have that much farther to go," I pointed out, trying to cheer them on.

"Who the hell do we have to screw to get a cool breeze around here?" said Jessica.

"Don't include me in that," I protested. "I'm too innocent to know about such things."

"Yeah, right, Mr. Jackhammer." Toff put a fist to his crotch and made rapid, obscene motions.

My whole neck felt as if it were burning with embarrassment. I looked around quickly and uneasily to see if any passing motorist or pedestrian was offended. No one seemed bothered by Toff's pantomime except me. Even Jessica laughed it off as she casually started checking text messages on her phone.

I punched Toff in the shoulder, knocking him off stride. "Stop that. You look like a perv."

Toff punched me back, hard. I grabbed my shoulder as a streak of pain shot through it. "Oww-wy," I groaned.

Then Toff and I grinned at each other, the affection open and easy between us.

"Oh my God," Jessica said, rolling her eyes as she fired off a text. "Why don't you two just make out already and get it over with?"

"I'M STARVING. Let's get something to eat."

I looked back at Toff and Jessica bringing up the rear as we emerged from the theater into the sunny, hot afternoon. My stomach growled for the entire last half of the movie, and I had a powerful craving for pizza, but mostly I wasn't ready to go home yet and wanted to keep hanging with my friends.

Toff shot a quick glance at Jessica, who said, "No, let's just head back to your house."

"But there's only fruit and nuts and salad fixings there," I replied, aware that I was whining like a little kid. "You know, healthy stuff. It's all my mom buys these days. Who wants that crap? *Geordi needs pizza.* Come on. The three of us ought to have enough cash to get a large sausage and cheese."

Jessica pulled out her phone. "I don't have any more cash on me. I left my wallet at your house." She started typing out a text message.

"Wallet?" I looked at her as if she'd said she'd left her head at my house. "What wallet? You never carried a wallet before."

"It was a gift from Toff. He just gave it to me today, right before we came to your house."

I looked at Toff, and his mouth was hanging open in what looked a lot like surprise. An instant later, he closed it, nodded solemnly, and said, "Yeah, that's right. I gave her the wallet… for her birthday, yeah."

"Jess's birthday isn't until next month," I pointed out.

"It was an early birthday present," Toff shot back.

"Whatever." They were obviously up to something, but I was too hungry to try figuring them out. I turned back to Jessica. "Toff and I can spring for the pizza. See? Problem solved."

Jessica looked at Toff. Toff coughed and looked at me. "Uh… well…." He seemed slightly embarrassed as his eyes shifted uneasily. "I spent all my money on the movie. And popcorn. You know how expensive that movie theater popcorn is. Sorry, dude."

"*Fine!*" I was in a huff. "I'll buy a small sausage and cheese pizza and we'll split it three ways." A third of a small pizza was barely a snack, but I was desperate for it. And although I could've claimed a bigger piece of the pie by virtue of funding the whole thing myself, it simply didn't feel right to do that to my friends. After all, I couldn't count the number of times Jessica and Toff had bought lunch or a movie ticket for me when I was short of cash. It was what we did for each other.

"Well…." Jessica hesitated as she read the response to the text message she'd just sent. She smiled, apparently pleased with the answer she'd gotten. "I think we need to put this to a vote. Show of hands. Who wants greasy, oily, artery-clogging, cardiac city, glue-cheesy, hard crusty, choke-on-it pizza?"

I felt my face go flat. "I'm guessing that's a 'no' from you, Jess."

"Aren't you smart, Geordi."

"I don't want pizza either," Toff added.

"Okay, I'm outvoted, then." *Argh!* "So what do you guys want to eat?"

Jessica appeared thoughtful for a moment. "You know, I could actually have a salad."

"Yeah. Me too," said Toff. "Topped off with some fruit and nuts."

"Now where can we get a snack like that?" Jessica looked up as if expecting the answer to write itself across the sky.

"*Fine!*" I snapped. "We'll go to my house!"

"Oooh. Grouchy." With the flat of her hand, Jessica whacked the back of my head.

"Cripes, Jess!"

"My, my. *Still* grouchy." She whacked me again, harder than before. "How do you feel now, Geordi?"

I clutched the back of my head and forced a grin that probably looked about as friendly as a shark's mouth. "I'm good."

"Wonderful!" Jessica threw one arm around my shoulders and the other around Toff's. "Let's go, pretty fellas."

WE REACHED my house roughly twenty minutes later, only a little sweaty and a bit out breath. For some reason the trip back didn't seem as arduous as the trip going.

"So what're we up to tonight?" I asked, leading the way across the lawn to the porch. "Video games at Jess's?"

"Nope. I'm burned out on games right now," Jessica replied right away. "Let's just watch TV or something."

Toff groaned. "Shit. The three of us seriously need some dates."

I felt relaxed and happy as I unlocked the front door and pushed it open. "Well, I'll ask Jess out," I said, looking back at Toff, "and she can ask you out, the three of us go out together, and voilà! Instant date."

I waited for Toff to respond, perhaps by kicking me not-so-playfully in the backside. I actually started to dodge away from him, but something ahead of me set off my alarms. There was a rush of movement from that direction, and my instincts told me to get the hell away. I flinched backward as I turned my head to face the oncoming menace, just as a shout blasted outward.

"*Surprise!*"

A short, stunned squeal yipped from my throat. "Oh, wow...."

There in the living room was my mom, both sets of grandparents, Aunt Rita and Uncle Ronnie, Aunt Jo and Uncle Milt, my four cousins, Carson Meyer, Jessica's mom and older brother, and six of my friends from the neighborhood. In the middle of this gathering stood my dad. Everyone was beaming at me as if I'd just found the cure for cancer while walking on water. All that adoration put a grin on my face as wide as the state of Tennessee.

Jessica nudged me in the back, urging me into the living room. Then she and Toff stepped inside, and Toff shut the door as my family and friends surged forward to hug me, pat me on the back, and otherwise congratulate me.

"We're so proud of you," said Aunt Rita.

"You go, Geordi!" said Uncle Milt.

"About time," growled Grandpa Percy. Grandpa Roland, Dad's dad, kind of stood back and scowled in his usual sourpuss mode.

"Oh, wow. Wow." I kept grinning, happy but confused. My birthday was last month, and my parents had treated me, Toff, and Jessica to a day of laser combat at Laser Zone, topped off with pizza, cake, and ice cream, exactly as I'd requested. A surprise party a whole month later was a total… well, surprise. My parents must not have wanted to break with the tradition of partying to commemorate the occasion of my earthly arrival. "Okay, you guys got me good," I said to Mom and Dad. "But we already celebrated my birthday."

"This isn't for your birthday," Dad said. Then he paused dramatically, waiting for me to get it.

I didn't get it. I could feel my grin start to freeze. "Uh…?"

Dad flung both of his arms out to his left, gesturing at something in that direction. I turned.

That's when I saw the huge, rainbow-colored banner that had somehow managed to escape my attention, hanging from the ceiling between the living room and dining room. It had a big picture of smiling me at the top, and below that, in bold, black letters, were the words, "Geordi Quintrell: Out of the Closet and Loving It!"

"*Happy coming-out day, Geordi!*" everybody shouted.

And then the voice of Diana Ross—the singer after whom my mom was named and whose songs my parents had played in heavy rotation for as long as I could remember—erupted from the house's sound system warbling, "I'm Coming Out."

My body went cold all the way down to my toes.

What the fu…?

LET'S BACK up for a bit.

Remember when Dad caught me doing the jack-handed solo to the sight of Corbin Bleu's naked butt? Dad considered my admission of the obvious as the moment I came out to my parents. Never mind that it was more a matter of my dad barging *into* the closet than me coming out of it. He wanted to commemorate the occasion, so the next day he faked Mom out and sneaked me away to my favorite five-star restaurant—Burger King—for dinner, and then we went to a movie.

Two weeks later, twelve-year-old Jessica took thirteen-year-old me up to the attic in her house and asked if we could make out.

She seemed uneasy about the idea herself, so I said, "Why do you want to do that?"

"My friend Teri made out with this guy from school. She says it was incredible and made her feel terrific. I don't want to miss out on incredible and terrific."

I'd never made out with anyone up to that point, and I didn't want to miss out on incredible and terrific either. Plus, I was just plain curious about the act. "Okay. Let's go for it."

We closed our eyes and kissed each other. Then Jessica took my hands and put them on her breasts. At the time, her chest was almost as flat as mine.

"Okay, we're through making out," Jessica announced and pushed my hands away from her. "Was it incredible and terrific?"

"Uh… no."

She looked hurt and confused.

"Jess, I'm gay," I added.

Jessica broke into a relieved smile, and I knew I'd made the right decision in telling her about my thing for boys. "Well, that explains it."

When I got home that evening, I told my parents I'd come out to Jessica (minus the part about making out).

"That's wonderful!" Mom and Dad exclaimed. Dad declared my coming out to a friend another cause for celebration, and he took the family out for ice cream and a few rounds of miniature golf.

There'd been no such celebrations since, because I never came out to anyone else.

So there I was two whole years later, at a surprise coming-out party thrown in my honor, with emphasis on the "surprise" portion. When I looked at Toff, he seemed just as shocked as I was.

One of my girl cousins tugged me into the open space between the living room and dining room, compelling me to dance with her to a second round of Diana Ross's "I'm Coming Out" while my two aunts clapped along. I tried my best to look happy, but I felt violated and cheated, although I didn't fully understand why. A steadily growing anger burned behind my smiling face. This party was my dad's doing. Sure, Mom helped, and obviously Jessica was in on it, but I knew without a doubt it was my dad's idea.

After my cousin and I finished dancing, I tried to get to Dad as he made a beeline for the kitchen. Carson Meyer intercepted me before I could follow.

"Hey, Geordi," he said, smiling at me in a serious sort of way. He was African American too, his skin maybe a shade lighter than my own. He was wearing loose, knee-length black athletic shorts, a white tank top, and sandals. God, who'd wear that to a party?

"Hey, Carson." I wanted to push past him, certain he was just going to taunt me in some slyly homophobic way, but my parents expected me to be polite, even to a not-exactly-a-friend-and-not-exactly-an-enemy like Carson. So I just stood there awkwardly with him, waiting for whatever came next.

Instead of being snide and snarky, Carson just looked a bit shy and a lot uneasy. He was now a few inches taller than me, and I hated that I was forced to look up at him. "So, uhm… gay, huh?" he said slowly. "You're really, like, gay."

"Yeah," I replied cautiously. "I am."

His smile widened. "I think you're a brave dude, man, coming out and all. You're braver than I'd be if I was gay. Gotta give it to ya. You're like, gay Superman." Then he reached over and gave me a pat on the back.

I was speechless for a few seconds after that. Even though I'd heard the words directly from Carson's mouth, part of me didn't want to believe he actually meant them. I kept waiting for the punchline, or an actual punch, to follow. Carson, with that admiring smile still on his face, ambled over to the table and poured himself a glass of ginger ale.

"Thanks, man," I finally mumbled to his back, feeling as good about myself as I did about that oozy sludge Mom made me wash out of our garbage bin every other week.

Suddenly, Dad came out of the kitchen at a rush, carrying a tray of tortilla chips and cheese dip. My attention refocused and I went after him. Tall and long-legged, Dad was moving so fast I had to run to catch up to him. "Dad, hold up—"

Uncle Ronnie came out of nowhere and intercepted me. "Here's the party boy," he said, his big booming voice rising over the music and chatter. He threw his arm around my shoulders. "Come here and let me talk to you."

"In a minute, Uncle Ronnie, okay?" I shrugged his arm off. "I need to talk something over with Dad."

"Aw, he's too busy for you right now. Come on with me. This won't take but a few minutes." He was Dad's older brother by something like a decade, gray-haired and cranky. He put his hands on my shoulders and guided me to a corner in the living room. "You know, the world sure has changed. When I was a kid and a young man, I didn't know a single gay person. Now gays are everywhere, on television, at church, in the sports bar. Hell, these days you can't swing a dead cat without hitting a gay in the face. You're not gonna be one of those gays who go around putting all your business in the street, are you, Nephew?"

"I'll try not to be, Uncle."

"I'm just wondering, what with you coming out and all. It's okay to keep some of your business to yourself, you know."

"Yeah, I know." I cut an annoyed glance at Dad as he offered the tray of chips and dip to my neighborhood friends. "Believe me, I know."

Dad began to move off with the tray. I started to pull away and follow, but Uncle Ronnie grabbed me by the arm and stopped me.

"Well now, here's something else that's got me concerned," Uncle Ronnie said. "When it comes to gay guys, I hear there's tops and there's bottoms. Are you a top or a bottom, Geordi? Please tell me you're not a bottom."

I frowned impatiently, confused. "I don't have an answer for that, Uncle. What's a top and what's a bottom? Explain it to me and then maybe I can answer you."

Uncle Ronnie suddenly looked as if he'd been punched in the gut. "Oh. I think your Aunt Rita is waving for me to come over. See you later, Nephew." He rushed off to where Aunt Rita was having a lively conversation with Jessica's mom.

Whatever.

Dad was in the dining room, making space for the chips and dip on the table, which was already crowded with platters of food. I started after him, determined to find out why he felt it necessary to force my gay side out to the world at large. I really wanted to ask him to stay out of my business, but I've never been particularly good at telling people off. Especially my parents.

Toff was standing just inside the dining room. As I started past him, he reached out and grabbed my arm.

"Just a second, Toff. I need to say something to my dad." I tried to shake off his hand.

Toff grabbed my arm tighter, and I turned to him, surprised. He looked hurt and angry.

"What is it?" I asked. "What's wrong?"

"I thought we were friends," he said.

"We *are* friends, Toff."

"Then why didn't you tell me?"

"Why didn't I tell you what?"

"That you're gay. You told everybody else. I'm your best friend, and I had to find out from a dumb sign." He gestured bitterly at the "Out of the Closet and Loving It" banner dangling from the ceiling behind us. The doorbell rang, and Dad hurried toward the front door, a big, welcoming grin already spreading across his face. In a flash of irritation, I started after him. He opened the door, and one of his coworkers from the museum walked in.

"Hey, Ben," said the coworker. He had a small, brightly wrapped gift in his hands. "Where's the kid of the hour?"

Dad looked around and spotted me coming up behind him. "There's His Majesty now," Dad said.

The coworker walked over to meet me. "Congratulations, Geordi, on your coming out. I picked up a little something for you to mark the occasion." He held out the gift to me.

I took the present, and part of me wanted to smile and offer thanks. At the same time, I wanted to grab Dad before he could take off again. And I thought of Toff, who was angry with me for reasons I didn't understand, and I wanted to find out what was going on with him. My brain must've short-circuited from all the conflicting impulses, because I froze for several moments and didn't do anything.

Then Toff took it upon himself to solve part of my dilemma. He ran past me and out the front door.

CHAPTER 3

As THE sun settled below the horizon and the western sky burned red-orange, I was sitting high in the branches of the big sugar maple tree just beyond the wooden fence at the edge of our backyard. The tree was in the yard of the neighbors who lived directly behind us. I'd been taking refuge in that tree since I was thirteen, whenever I needed privacy from my dad.

The neighbors, Mr. and Mrs. Caple, a retired couple in their seventies, were home. I caught a glimpse of their silhouettes, sitting in front of the TV in their family room, right after I'd climbed into the tree. I was pretty sure they were aware of my periodic trespassing, but they never said anything to me or, as far as I knew, my parents. Maybe they understood that I needed a getaway every now and then.

I watched a jet soaring over the horizon. It was so far away and so high up it looked like a silvery dot skimming lazily along, leaving a cloud-like tendril of white condensation behind it. I wondered what it was like to be the pilot, shut away in a cockpit close to the edge of space with the world turning distantly below you. No one could get to you up there.

Something rustled softly below. The sound grew louder as someone climbed up into the tree. I didn't bother to look down. Other than the Caples, only two people knew of my hideout, and one of them apparently wasn't talking to me now.

Jessica pulled herself up and sat on the massive branch across from me, her feet dangling. "Figured you'd be up here," she said. "Your mom and dad are looking for you."

"Tell me something I don't know. They've been blowing up my cell phone."

"It's kind of rude to duck out of a party when you're the guest of honor."

"So shoot me." I turned to her. "I had to get out of that place. This is probably not gonna make any sense, considering all the people in the house are my family and friends, but I started feeling really lonely in there."

Jessica nodded. "I've felt that way too, when I'm around people who just don't get me. My brother never gets me." She pulled a pear from her pocket and bit into it.

"Toff got mad at me and walked out of the party. And before you ask, I didn't do anything to him. I don't know why he's so pissed at me."

"I do."

I waited for her to explain, but she just sat there chewing down a mouthful of pear. "Well? You gonna enlighten me or you want me to pay you first?"

"He's angry because you didn't tell him you're into boys. I know because, just before he got in your face, he told me how hurt he felt that you hid something like that from him."

I grew even more annoyed. "Well, that's just dumb. I didn't personally come out to most of the people at that fick-facking party, and none of them got all whiny about it. What's the big deal? It's not like Toff was gonna date me or anything if he'd known earlier."

Jessica chomped another plug out of the pear. "Come on, Geordi. You said you and Toff have been friends since you were seven. That's a long time, like half our lives. Be honest. If Toff had dyslexia or something but never told you, and you only found out by accident, how would you feel?"

The answer became clear to me instantly. "I'd feel like he didn't trust me, like maybe our friendship wasn't as tight as I thought it was."

"Exactly."

"Shit. I'm a rotten person."

"If it helps any, you should know that Toff's angry with me too. He asked if I knew you were gay, and I told him you came out to me when I was twelve. So he's pissed that I knew and didn't tell him."

"Well, why *didn't* you fill him in?"

"I thought that was your story to tell, not mine."

If only Dad felt that way.... "But Toff must've known about me before the party. He helped you get me away from the house, and then he helped you get me back home when I wanted us to hang out and eat pizza."

"Your parents just told us to get you out of the house so they could set up for a surprise party, and they texted me to make sure we got you back in three hours. Toff and I just assumed it was gonna be a regular party. They didn't say anything about you coming out. Maybe they thought you'd already told Toff and me since the three of us are so close." She shrugged. "They were half right, anyway."

I pulled out my phone and fired off a text to Toff, something I'd already done several times since taking refuge in the tree. Toff never turned off his phone in the summer and, unless he was asleep, he'd always text me back right off. I waited a whole minute, staring at the screen on my phone. "Toff still won't answer." I sighed. "Maybe I should go by his house—"

"I wouldn't do that, not right now," Jessica said quickly. "Maybe you should just give him some time to cool off."

"Come on, Jess. He can't be *that* pissed over me not coming out to him."

"It's not just that. You know things aren't that good for Toff. Your parents are always making a fuss over you, throwing parties for you, taking you on trips. My mom goes overboard doing stuff for me and my brother. Next month is my quinceañera, and Mom's making a huge deal out of that. All Toff has is his dad, and his dad barely acknowledges Toff's alive. I think your parents throwing this surprise coming-out party really got to Toff."

An ache shot through me, making me even more anxious to go to Toff's house and patch things up between us. And my general sense of aggravation found a single focus. "This is all my dad's fault."

Jess rolled her eyes. "You think every bad thing in the world is your dad's fault."

"That's because every bad thing in the world *is* my dad's fault."

She threw her pear core at me, which would have hit me smack in the middle of my forehead if I hadn't ducked. I watched as it dropped to the ground. "Hey. That's littering," I protested.

"You shouldn't have ducked," said Jessica. "Besides, it's biodegradable." She reached over and patted me on the knee. "Come on. Let's get you back to your party."

"Can you do a brother a favor and just stab me instead?"

"Not this time. Your dad sent me to find you. I think he's kinda expecting me to bring you back alive." She slipped off the branch so suddenly it scared me, dropping down to snag a lower branch with her hands. She hung for a moment, feet dangling about eight feet off the ground. With a kick of both legs, she swung her body back and then forward, letting go of the branch at the apex of her outward swing and dropping to the ground. She touched down on the grass with all the quiet, nimble grace of a cat landing on its feet.

Not to be outdone, I slid off the branch intending to drop feetfirst onto the same lower branch, jump off, and reach the ground in an Olympic-style landing. My feet slipped on the lower branch as if it had been slathered with oil, and then I slammed down on my butt and bounced into the air. I struck my head on the underside of the upper branch, hit the lower branch again, this time on my left hip, and fell heavily to the ground, landing flat on my back. Somebody screamed just about the whole time I was falling. I'm pretty sure it was me.

"Geordi!"

My eyes were closed, and the sound of Jessica's shouts were kind of muffled. I think I was a little stunned for a few seconds. I felt her kneel anxiously beside me. "Jeez. Are you okay? Geordi?" She put her hands on my shoulder and shook me. "Are you hurt?"

My back, left hip, and the top of my head ached like crazy, so yeah, I was definitely hurt. But I was ten times more embarrassed than hurt. I kept thinking, *Jessica saw me tumble out of a tree like a fool, and she's never gonna let that go. She'll tell all our friends. I won't be able to show my face anywhere without somebody pointing me out to some little kid and going, "That's the overgrown idiot who fell out of a tree. Don't be stupid like him."*

"Geordi?" She shook me harder. "Say something or I'm calling 911."

"Am I dead?"

"Well… no."

Dag.

IN THE kitchen Mom was stirring up a fresh pitcher of lemonade. She froze when I walked through the door. "What on earth happened to you?"

"Oh… nothing."

She came over to me. "Look at you, Geordi," she said, frowning in concern as she brushed her hand over my head. The party was still going strong: I could hear laughter and music rumbling from the living room. "You've got tree bark in your hair. Your shirt's ripped. There are grass stains all over the back of your pants. And that bruise on your arm…. Geordi, what on earth—"

"I was just playing a little football with the guys, Mom. No big deal." I pulled away from her. Every time she stroked my hair, the top of my head flared with hot pain. It was a wonder she didn't feel the lump that had swollen dead center over my skull.

Mom has a bullshit meter like nothing in this world. It puts lie detectors to shame, and if she could figure out a way to package and market it, she'd be a trillionaire. She gave me her I-know-you're-lying-through-your-teeth look. "No, you weren't playing football. Tell me what *really* happened. I know it has something to do with a tree. You got freaky in a tree, didn't you? And you got so caught up you fell out of the tree on your little narrow behind—"

"Oh-*kay* Mom. Nice chatting with you. I'm gonna change clothes and get back to the party."

"Smart choices, son," she said to my back as I rushed out of the kitchen. "I keep telling you to make smart choices when it comes to your life."

I locked myself in my room. *Thanks a lot, Dad.* If he hadn't thrown that stupid party, Toff wouldn't be mad at me. If he hadn't sent Jessica after me, I wouldn't have bounced my butt out of that tree in front of her. With anger steaming in my head, I got into a fresh pair of jeans and the "Progressive Tennessean" T-shirt Mom brought back from her teachers' conference in Nashville last month. The idea of pulling the shades and hiding under my bed was mighty tempting, but Jessica had probably told Dad I was back already. If I didn't show my face, he'd come down and personally escort me back to the party.

I put on a smile and walked into the living room. None of the guests had left, much to my regret. In fact, even more people seemed to be present. There was Jake Butcher, the son of my dad's boss, dancing with my cousin Mae. I'd known him since we were eight years old. We hung out maybe three or four times a year, usually at museum functions. Jake was now a tall, buff, and mighty good-looking brother. Mae was staring at him as if she wanted to stick her tongue all the way down to his stomach. As handsome as he was, I personally would never kiss Jake. He used to swallow live bugs on a dare and, knowing him, he probably still did. I'm not keen on the idea of putting my tongue anywhere bugs have been crawling. Just saying.

And there was Caitlin Eisner. Her family moved into town about seven months ago, and she and Jessica took to each other right off.

Caitlin was blonde and pretty. She was also, as my Uncle Ronnie would put it, "pleasingly plump." She was over in a corner of the dining room, holding hands with Jessica and laughing as they danced away.

They were all girly as they dipped and stepped and twirled, letting go of each other when they went into their spins but joining hands again once they were face-to-face. Jessica looked cool in her cut-off jeans and tank top, and Caitlin looked like hot-spun cotton candy in her fuzzy pink sundress. Caitlin leaned forward and tiptoed to whisper something in Jess's ear. Jess laughed out loud and squeezed Caitlin's shoulder.

I felt a twinge of jealousy. Jessica really seemed to like Caitlin.

"Hey, Geordi."

I turned, a bit startled. Jake was standing close behind me. Smiling.

It was a damn pretty smile. Nice, moist lips. Lots of sparkly white teeth. He'd ditched the Afro he usually wore, his hair buzzed down close to his beautifully shaped head, and his dark brown skin was positively glowing.

Dark. Brown. Skin.

Glowing.

"Oh… uh…." I often went "Oh" and "Uh" when all the blood in me went running south of the border, leaving my brain high and dry. My groin suddenly felt heavy. "Hi, Jake." I looked up into his genial auburn eyes. Jeez, everybody was turning into giants. Jake was almost as tall as Jessica now. Toff was the only friend I had who was still stuck at five foot seven like me. Damn. Jake somehow was even better-looking than he was when I saw him five minutes ago.

Jake put his hands on his hips, which had the effect of broadening his shoulders and making his pecs flex delightfully beneath the fabric of his sleeveless red T-shirt. A few weeks ago, I overheard his dad tell my dad that Jake had started weight training so he could try out for his school's wrestling team in the fall. The training was definitely showing. "So. You're out and loving it, huh?" he asked.

"Uh… oh, you know…." I grinned as I slid my hand in my pocket and pinched my thigh hard, again and again. It was the only way to stop the spread of a boner down my leg. My thought processes seemed to have ground to a halt. What was it about being around hot, handsome dudes that just sucked all the oxygen out of my brain?

He grinned back at me. My grin probably looked stupid. His grin looked sexy. My crotch got heavy again. *This can't be happening. I can't*

*be getting turned on by Jake freaking Butcher. Please God, don't do this
to me.*

"I never would've thought you were gay, man," Jake said. "You're
full of surprises."

"Surprises, yeah. Me. Full of."

He gave me a one-eyed squint. Or was it—oh jeez—a wink? "You
know, I might have a surprise or two in me."

"Oh?" That came out more like a gasp. What happened to all the
air in this room?

"Ever dance with a guy before?"

That got me so excited I thought the top of my sore head would
spin off. "N-no."

He stepped back, made a bow, and held out his hand to me. "Then
let me be your first."

Cue the theme from *The Twilight Zone.*

I was stunned. This was absolutely and totally unreal, so unreal I
just stood there staring at Jake. He smiled and took my hand and pulled
me out into the middle of the living room. Thankfully, a fast song was
playing. If it had been a slow song and I'd gone front to front with Jake,
I don't think shoving a machete through my thigh would have been
enough to stop me from throwing wood.

Jake was a great dancer, those long ropy arms and legs popping and
locking hypnotically. After I stopped being stunned, I turned out some
pretty good moves myself. The jeans Jake had on were just tight enough to
be *Thank-ya-Jesus-hallelujah!* enticing, and I was equally happy whether
he turned his back, front, or either side to me as we danced. My other guests
gathered around and clapped to the music, urging us on. Mom and Dad
actually cheered. Mae didn't seem especially happy for us, though. She
gave me such an evil eye I thought she wanted to set fire to my hair.

But I was more taken with the way Jake looked at me. His gaze and
his smile were so warm they made me tingle inside. His expression held
a world of meaning, and all of it flowed right into making me feel like a
pretty special guy. How could someone do that with just his eyes and his
lips? How could a guy go from being a bug eater to a freaking hot-bod?
How could I get myself out of this dance with my dignity intact?

That last question was especially relevant, because every time I
looked at Jake's mouth, I had to fight the urge to send my tongue on a
bug chase.

IT TOOK two whole hours after Jessica hauled my sorry butt back home for my coming-out party to end. I spent much of that time worrying about Toff. He was pretty upset when he left, and I started getting afraid that he'd never talk to me again.

But there were distractions that took my mind off those worries. After the song ended, Jake actually thanked me for letting him be my first boy dance partner. *He* thanked *me*! And then he gave me a congratulatory hug, whispering "Happy coming-out day, Geordi" in my ear before moving off to mingle with the other guests. I mingled too but always seemed to find my way back into visual range of Jake. He never freaked out or anything when he caught me looking at him; he just winked or smiled. And every time he winked or smiled, it felt as if I were levitating.

It occurred to me that I really didn't know that much about Jake, a circumstance I suddenly wanted to change. Was he gay? He did say he might have a surprise or two in him. Could he be getting ready to come out himself? Would he hang out with me, maybe go on a date with me, if I asked? Maybe I'd have worked up the nerve to ask him out if he hadn't gone right back to hanging with Mae after chatting with my other cousins. Dag, what was up with the dude? Mae was sixteen and stacked like a brick house, so hanging with her was definitely straight-guy behavior. But there was nothing straight about those winks and smiles he shot my way.

When the party ended and my guests started to leave, I stood at the front door the way Mom always insisted to send everyone off with a personal thanks-for-coming and goodbye. When Jake headed out after his dad, he stopped and shook my hand. "Great party, man," he said, flashing that newly knee-weakening smile of his.

"I'm glad you had a good time, Jake. Thanks for coming." We'd finished shaking hands, but Jake held on, looking into my eyes. His grip was so warm, so strong. Alluring. Breathtaking. *Jeez*.... Uncomfortable, I lowered my gaze and found myself looking at his crotch. "Oh... uh...."

He laughed in that way parents do when their baby babbles something cute. "See you around, Geordi." Then he squeezed my hand, let go, and hurried out to his dad's car. I closed the door, holding my Jake-squeezed hand up like it was a delicate piece of glass.

I turned around and almost bumped into Mom, who had just walked up behind me. "Well," she said cheerily, "that was a wonderful celebration."

"Uh-huh."

"You and Jake certainly seemed to enjoy each other."

"Yeah. I like Jake."

Mom gave me that hopeful look, and I knew what she'd ask next. "Is that as in *like* like, or just plain like?" Dad was hovering in the dining room, gathering dirty paper plates into a garbage bag. I could tell he was listening eagerly for my answer.

My parents are as progressive as can be. Mom teaches fifth grade at our neighborhood elementary school—she walks to work, rain or shine, claiming that's good for her health and the environment—and Dad is the director of the Education Department at the Pink Palace Museum. They believe unequivocally in recycling, equality, socialism, green energy, universal healthcare, a woman's right to choose, a living wage for all, and the complete and utter separation of church and state. Since finding out about my gay side, they'd been anxious for me to begin embracing my identity. They were probably more ready for me to have a boyfriend than I was.

I'd never kissed a guy, held a guy in my arms, gone out on a date or made out with a guy. I'd never had a boyfriend. I wanted to experience all those things, and yes, I now would have liked very much to start experiencing them with Jake. But Jake and his parents lived in Arlington, a quiet, rural, fast-growing town in the northeastern section of Shelby County. That was a pretty long haul from Midtown Memphis, where my parents and I lived in the hip, historic, and very gay friendly Cooper-Young district. As things stood, I probably wouldn't see Jake again until October, when the museum put on its annual Crafts Fair. We'd never exchanged cell phone numbers, so I couldn't even text or call him.

I could have pumped Dad for information about Jake. I could have also gotten Dad to pass on a message through Jake's father for Jake to call me. I was still pissed with Dad, however. Looking at him made my eyes burn, and I didn't want to have anything to do with him just yet. And even if Jake and I texted or hit each other up on Facebook or Snapchat or whatever, hanging out with him would never be as simple as just walking over to his house, the way I did with Toff, Jess, and the rest of my friends. So there wasn't any point in trying to pursue any type of relationship with the dude.

"No, Mom," I answered, "I just plain like him."

Mom looked disappointed. That made two of us.

CHAPTER 4

TOFF IS a phenomenal guy and a great friend, and I am a selfish bastard.

Toff proved himself phenomenal on the very first day we met. It was a cool and sunny Saturday morning in spring after a nearly weeklong spell of windy rain showers. I was seven, and I'd gotten Mom to put me into my rain boots so I could go out and stomp my way through all the puddles in our neighborhood. I wound up in a big lot that had been cleared and graded for the construction of a new house. There were lots of puddles—*muddy* puddles. I thought I'd made it to heaven.

There was a girl in our neighborhood who was big for a nine-year-old. She would have been big for a nineteen-year-old, or at least I thought so at the time. Her name was Belle, but some smartass nicknamed her Big Belle, which evolved into Big Bull. Looking back on it all now, I can understand how a girl widely known as Big Bull would be self-conscious and a little miserable, and how that would keep her in an almost perpetual state of being pissed off. But at seven, I thought Belle was just plain mean.

I had my head down, merrily splish-splashing my way across that muddy lot when suddenly I came up against a wall. That's what it felt like when I bumped into Belle. She stood there with her arms at her sides, staring down at me as if the mere fact that I was having fun offended her. She didn't say a word, just casually reached out and shoved me butt-first into the mud. She waited patiently while I struggled to my feet and then shoved me down again.

There was no fighting Belle. Other kids tried and lost. Badly. I'd tried myself, a couple of weeks before, when she knocked my backpack off my shoulder and I punched her in the stomach for it. She responded by picking me up and slamming my back against a wood fence. I think my body and that fence twanged for fifteen minutes from the impact.

I wasn't about to repeat that mistake, so after my second trip down into the mud, I figured it was best to just lie there until Belle decided to move on and darken someone else's day. Obviously she still saw potential for torment, however; she started kicking the thick brown watery sludge over my whole body as if trying to make me into the world's biggest mud pie. I lay there and cried. Really, what else could I do?

Then I heard this high-pitched little voice shouting, "No fair! No fair! Leave him alone!" Toff came running from out of nowhere. He got between me and Belle, and he did one of the bravest things I thought anybody could ever do. He planted his little hands against Belle's shoulders and pushed her back.

Or, I should say, he *tried* to push her back. Toff was as small and thin as I was. He stood as much chance of pushing Belle away as he did of buying the Empire State Building for cash. But he kept pushing and pushing until Belle, who was looking pretty bored by then, planted a hand on his forehead and shoved him down in the mud next to me.

Belle walked away. I'd stopped crying, amazed by what Toff had done. Toff and I looked at each other. "Are you okay?" he asked.

"Yeah."

"I'm Sandor."

"I'm Geordi. Wanna come to my house? My mom's making tofu burgers for lunch."

"Okay."

See what I mean about Toff being phenomenal? How many kids do you know who'd risk their own butts to help another kid who's getting slaughtered by a bully? How many kids do you know who'd risk their stomachs eating a tofu burger? Toff had just moved into the neighborhood with his dad—Belle moved out of town with her family a couple of weeks later, which seemed a pretty decent tradeoff to me—so he didn't even know me when he rushed to my rescue. That made him my friend right off. Mud mates for life, yeah!

Over the years, Toff had shown the depth of his friendship in dozens of ways, including:

1) Standing up to Mr. Hanson, our elementary school principal, when the man falsely accused me of deliberately belching out a moose mating call to disrupt his announcements during afternoon assembly. It *was* an accident, by the way. I'd had two Pepsis for lunch.

2) Hiding a three-foot ice sculpture of a snowman in his father's deep freezer for four days so Dad and I could surprise my mom with it on Christmas Day. She said her parents had one every Christmas when she was growing up.

3) Giving me a giant Snickers bar every year on my birthday. I love Snickers, but Mom won't buy them—or anything else that a human being might actually enjoy snacking on. Thank God Dad did all the menus for my parties.

4) Using his emergency cash to buy me four new sets of underwear from the commissary at summer camp after I accidentally burned all my tighty-whities trying to light a fire for roasting hot dogs. Don't ask me how that happened. Just… don't ask.

And I repaid all that devotion by being a selfish bastard. What else would you call it? After my coming-out party, I didn't spend the night worrying about Toff feeling hurt and left out. No, I spent the night fantasizing about all the ways I wanted to kiss Jake Butcher. Every time I thought of kissing Jake, Toff's face popped into my head and dumped buckets of guilt all over my brain. By Sunday morning, I was so disgusted with myself, I couldn't even eat breakfast. I decided it was time to make amends with Toff. If he'd even speak to me, that is.

The Tofflers and the Quintrells were not churchgoers, so Sunday morning was as good a time to make my apologies to Toff as any. I'd usually text before I dropped in on one of my friends, but in this instance I thought showing up out of the blue was the best strategy. I walked the two blocks to his house under a sunny sky, already sweltering in the hot, humid air. At Toff's house, I knocked quietly on the door. A few seconds later, Mr. Toffler opened the door.

"Geordi," he said with a nod. Mr. Toffler wasn't a big man, only an inch or two taller than me with a wiry body almost like a kid's. His face was heavily lined, though. He wore his hair long, and he had a beard. His hair and beard were streaked with gray, and he looked more like sixty-five than forty-five. Mr. Toffler's eyes always seemed to be focused somewhere else, even when he stared directly at you. He never looked happy or sad or upset or anything. In all the years I'd been coming to this house, I'd never seen him even smile. It was easy to believe he didn't feel anything.

"Hi, Mr. Toffler," I said, flashing a little smile. "I came to see—"

"Sandor!" he bellowed over his shoulder, not waiting for me to finish. "Geordi's here!" He turned back to me, stepping aside as he did so. "He's in the kitchen. Go on back."

"Thanks." I walked inside, crossed the living room and dining room, and turned left into the kitchen. Toff was at the stove frying bacon. On the counter next to him was a plate holding two slices of bread slathered with mayo and piled high with lettuce, sliced tomato, and pickles. Mmm, a BLT. That sounded and smelled heavenly compared to the granola with almond milk and sliced fruit that Mom set out in front of me for breakfast. The moment I walked into Toff's kitchen, my appetite sat up and begged like a hungry dog.

But I was through being a selfish bastard and pushed away all thought of asking Toff to share his sandwich. "Hey." *Please say it back. Please, please, please don't leave me hanging.*

"Hey, Geordi." He didn't turn to me, and he sounded sort of sad. But at least he was speaking to me.

Sighing inwardly, I sat down at the table. "Can we talk? It can wait until after you have your breakfast if you want."

"No, we can talk now. The bacon has to finish cooking." He turned, came to the table, and sat down across from me. He was barefoot, wearing only a pair of blue striped, knee-length pajama bottoms, and his hair was sticking out all over his head. Calmly, he folded his hands together on the table in front of him and waited.

Now that I was there, I wasn't sure exactly how to start. Before I could pull my head together, Mr. Toffler called out, "I'm leaving now, Sandor. Be sure to lock up if you take off before I get back."

"Okay, Dad," Toff called back.

I heard the front door close. "So where's your dad off to?" That was so not what I wanted to ask.

"Shelby Farms," Toff said. "He's going fishing. He likes to go by himself." And then he sat there, waiting for me to say my piece.

Okay. Just go ahead and lay it out there. "Toff, I'm really sorry I got you so upset yesterday. And I get it. I understand why you were mad that I didn't tell you before that I'm gay—"

"Wait, wait a second," said Toff, a look of pain and… something else suddenly crossing his face. "You don't have to apologize. I shouldn't have gotten so mad at you."

"No, it's okay, man. You were right to be pissed off. You're one of my closest friends, and I shouldn't have kept that part of my life from you. But not telling you about being gay didn't have anything to do with me not trusting you. It was about me. I'm still trying to figure all this stuff out, you know, trying to understand these feelings I'm having. And sometimes I feel some pretty weird stuff." Like suddenly getting hot for Jake Butcher, but I didn't want to say that to Toff. "My parents keep sticking their noses in all this, especially my dad, and that just complicates things for me and makes it so much harder. But I don't want to make excuses. Not telling you was wrong, and I'm really sorry."

Now Toff looked as if he was about to cry or something. He blinked and shook his head.

"Just don't give up on me, okay," I rambled on, afraid Toff had already decided to write off our friendship. Why else would he look so teary-eyed? "You're a big part of my life, and I don't want to lose that. Ever. I love you, man. I really do."

Toff's eyes got wide, and he froze. Then he shot up from his chair so fast I thought something in the house had caught fire. I stood up too. Next moment he rushed around the table, and I was surprised to have his arms around me. I was even more surprised when Toff said, "Jesus, Geordi," and squeezed his now tear-sparkled eyes shut and kissed me dead on the mouth.

Huh? What?

The term "seismic shift" alludes to the severe and widespread destruction of the landscape brought about by a big earthquake. The phrase is often used to describe a sudden, profound, and far-reaching alteration of a particular state of affairs.

Toff's kiss was a seismic shift.

Stunned is not strong enough to describe what that kiss did to me. I just stood there at first because my mind simply couldn't process entirely what was happening. *Gay. Toff is* gay. After a few moments, the kiss going on and on with no end in sight, my senses started to register certain things. Toff's lips felt warm and very soft. His skin smelled lemony, probably from the soap he used in his shower. His hair looked shiny and damp, a stunted, spiky brown forest sprouting over his scalp. And his mouth tasted of cool, snappy mint. Another feeling, vague and elusive, lurked below my senses.

I also felt the passion behind the kiss, the strong emotion that powered it. I didn't know what to make of that. It caused me more and more discomfort, however, as the kiss seemed to take on a life of its own. Toff was squeezing me hard in his arms. I wanted to push him away. I wanted him off me so I could catch my breath and figure out exactly what was happening here. But if I pushed him away, if that hurt his feelings…. No, I couldn't hurt him again. I just couldn't do that to him. I stood there and let the kiss go on.

Finally Toff broke away and pushed himself back, holding me by the shoulders as he peered deeply into my eyes. He was smiling. His face, streaked with tears, looked as innocent and sweet as it did when we were seven.

And I felt as dazed as if I'd been bashed in the head with a brick.

"Geordi, I'm sorry too," Toff said in a rushed and breathless voice. "I shouldn't have gotten mad at you yesterday. I was hurt because I've had feelings for you for a whole year now, and I didn't know, I didn't have a clue, that you could feel the same way about me. So I didn't say anything and just hoped the feelings would go away. But they didn't, and they kept getting stronger until it hurt to be around you. And then yesterday, when I found out you were gay too, it made me angry to think of all the time that was lost when we could have maybe been closer. I wasn't actually mad at you. I was angry with myself for not telling you way before yesterday how I felt about you. And now, to hear that you're in love with me too…."

Wait. What—?

Before I could say or do anything, he pulled me in and kissed me again.

Did I hear that right? Did Toff just say he was *in* love with me?

Fresh tears streaming down his face, Toff laughed and mumbled in between kisses, "You've just made me so happy, Geordi. Nobody's ever made me this happy."

Yup, he was in love with me.

Dag.

BAD THINGS happen to everybody; that's just the way life goes. Jessica's dad walked away from his family when she was twelve. That sucked, definitely, but you know what? The whole Sanchez family was in better shape after that departure, including Mr. Sanchez.

The man was an alcoholic. I remember the first time I saw him, when I was nine, not long after Jess and I had become friends. We were in her living room on a cloudy Friday afternoon in October, lying on the floor and playing a game of Uno. We were loud and having fun, going "In your face!"

or "Eat this!" every time we played a Draw Two, Reverse, Skip, or Draw Four card.

Then Mr. Sanchez walked through the front door, and Jess went completely still. He drifted past us like a robot, leaving an acrid smell in his wake that I'd later come to call whiskey fumes. Jess gathered up the cards, as in game over. "We have to be quiet now."

Spunky. Mom said that was her impression of Jessica when I introduced them to each other. Nobody intimidated Jess. I didn't even think Belle could have done that if she'd still been part of the neighborhood when Jess moved in. But Jess's dad did it just by walking through the room. Now *that* was scary.

None of my other friends were afraid of their parents. It made me afraid for Jess. "What's wrong?" I asked.

"If we stay in the house, we have to be quiet," Jess replied. Her whole face had shut down, as blank as a television screen that had been turned off. Mr. Sanchez's drunkenness sucked all the life out of her. "My dad doesn't like to hear noise when…."

"When what?" I asked, but Jess never answered. She didn't have to. By the time I left her house that day, I'd learned that Mr. Sanchez couldn't stand any noise when he was drunk. Noise made him pugnacious, made him go off like a cannon. But whether the noise was Jess and her brother talking loudly or the neighbor's dog barking incessantly or a car horn blowing in the street, Mr. Sanchez always yelled and cussed at Mrs. Sanchez.

After three years of that, Mrs. Sanchez finally got fed up and told her husband to leave. Mr. Sanchez didn't put up any resistance. Mrs. Sanchez told him all the cussing and yelling wasn't good for their children, and Mr. Sanchez loved his children more than anything. So despite having a belligerent drunk for a father, Jess at least knew her dad gave a damn about her.

Toff wasn't so lucky.

Toff's mother died in a traffic accident; he was only two years old at the time. She was in the passenger seat when Mr. Toffler drove their car into the path of a freight train. It was night, the crossing gates and lights malfunctioned, and Mr. Toffler didn't know the train was approaching. The impact crushed the passenger side and shoved the car half a mile down the track before the engineer could stop the train. Toff learned all this from newspaper accounts of the accident. His father never talked to him about it.

Toff said he doesn't remember his mom at all. His father never told him anything about her, even when he begged, even when he cried and cussed and demanded to know. Toff thought his dad did cocaine for years after his mother died. He remembered seeing his dad sniff white powder off the back of his hand. At the time Toff thought the powder was medicine because the only times his father seemed to brighten up and come alive was after he'd had a snort. A few years ago, Toff's dad sent him off to live with a cousin—now deceased—in Portland for six months. Toff was sure his dad was in rehab during that time. After he returned home, Toff never saw his dad snorting white powder again. He also never saw his dad energized again.

Mr. Toffler seemed distracted, his mind working perpetually away at a problem that could never be solved. He kept food in the house, paid the light, gas, and water bills on time, provided clothes for Toff. If Toff asked for something specific—art supplies, new shoes, a solar system model for a school project, money for the movies—Mr. Toffler gave it to him. But he never gave Toff what Toff wanted most.

Attention.

For everything outside of his material needs, Toff had to find a surrogate. His dad just didn't work that way.

My dad taught Toff how to ride a bike, picked him up when he fell, bandaged his wounds, and patted him on the back.

My mom helped Toff with his homework and school projects, comforted him when he was sad or afraid, and told him what a smart boy he was.

Mrs. Sanchez answered Toff's questions about life, love, and sex, showed him how to make his favorite sandwich (the BLT), and taught him how to tie a four-in-hand knot for our middle-school graduation ceremony.

Toff tried mightily to make a connection with his dad. At first it was because he really wanted the man to be proud of him. But it got to a point where he would have settled for having his dad just freaking *notice* him. In school he worked hard and brought home straight As. Not that it meant shit to his father.

The first grading period when we were in fourth grade is a perfect example of what I mean. Toff and I walked home from school the day report cards went out, and I could see the hope in his face. Mr. Toffler was sitting in the chair in the living room with the newspaper open on his lap, staring at the wall. His gaze shifted to the paper when Toff and I walked in, as if he'd been reading all along.

"Hi, Dad." Hope sent a shaky smile spreading across Toff's face.

"Hi, Sandor. Hello, Geordi." Mr. Toffler's voice was about as lively as a broken toaster. It gave me a bad feeling for Toff. I could see it as plainly as writing on a chalkboard; nothing good was coming out of this.

"Guess what, Dad. It's report card day." Toff put down his backpack, ran over to his dad's chair, and grabbed his dad's cell phone from the table. He was about to pull up email when his dad reached out and, without a word, took the phone from him.

Toff's hopeful smile faded. His voice got quiet. "But… I want you to see my report card, Dad."

"Not now," Mr. Toffler said.

"I got As in everything. Everything. And Mrs. Tripplehorne says I'm one of the best students she's got. She says it right there on the report card. You gotta see it."

"There's egg salad in the fridge," Mr. Toffler replied, apparently having an entirely different conversation. "You can make yourself a sandwich for dinner."

I still remember the look of hurt on Toff's face.

He did that for years, personally showing—or trying to, anyway—his dad every report card the teachers emailed because otherwise his dad would never open them. He might as well have shown his grades to a wall.

When good grades didn't get him what he wanted, Toff got mad and stopped everything: studying, turning in homework, taking tests. He even quit the basketball team, which he'd just made only a few months earlier. His grades dropped so drastically the teachers called his dad to express their concerns directly. Mr. Toffler didn't get angry, didn't demand to know what the hell was going on with Toff, didn't tell him those grades better come up or else. He just hung up after each call and let his mind wander back into its faraway mode. It was my mom who got upset with Toff, told him he was letting himself down, that doing his best was more important than anything his father did or did not do. It was my mom who got him to bring his grades up again.

But the saddest thing that happened to Toff after the death of his mother was this: Last year, in May, Toff, Jess, and I were walking home from the movie theater in Overton Square when we spotted two old men eating bread and fruit from the dumpster behind the neighborhood supermarket. Jess walked right up and asked why they were doing that. We learned that the shelter where the men took refuge occasionally had run short of funds and correspondingly cut meals for its residents down to one a day. The men took food from the dumpster to make up for the two meals they'd lost.

Jess talked to the supermarket's manager. The produce and bread in the dumpster wasn't moldy or rotten or anything. The items had just reached the limit set by the store's freshness guidelines without selling and were discarded. Jess then talked with the director of the homeless shelter and the store manager on a three-way call and worked out an agreement to send the store's outdated bread, fruits, and vegetables to the shelter. Toff organized a car wash at one of the gas stations on Union Avenue with me, Jess, and some of the other kids from school. That car wash raised almost a thousand dollars for the homeless shelter.

Jess's and Toff's efforts caught the attention of the media and the mayor. The mayor set up a ceremony at city hall to honor all the kids who worked to help the shelter. Jess and Toff were singled out for leading the charge. Toff told his dad and begged him to come. Mr. and Mrs. Sanchez were there, together, even though they were divorced by that time. My mom and dad were there. All the other kids' parents were there. Even the school principal and several of our teachers were there.

But not Mr. Toffler.

Toff came home with me after the ceremony because he couldn't stand to go to his own house. He went straight to the patio where he stood in his suit and four-in-hand tie, staring out into the backyard as he held his Certificate of Appreciation for Meritorious Service to the Citizens of Memphis loosely in his left hand. I walked out there and stood next to him. I could tell he was hurt, and I didn't want him to be alone. I didn't have a clue what to say to the guy and was incapable of taking away his pain, but I could at least make damn sure he knew he wasn't alone.

"Nothing I do matters," he said.

"That's not true, Toff, and you know it."

"Nothing I do matters to *him*." The certificate slipped from his fingers and blew across the lawn in the wind. In this very quiet voice, Toff said, "You know, Geordi, sometimes I wish my dad would just die."

"Don't say that!"

"He might as well be dead. He sure as shit isn't living. And I'm alone whether he's there or not." Toff started crying, his weeping soft and almost silent. I sat down on the patio with him and held my arm around his shoulders, and he cried for a very long time.

THAT WAS then. Now I stood in Toff's kitchen Sunday morning and let him kiss me and hug me and kiss me some more. He stopped only when smoke began to roll up from the stove.

"Oh shit! I'm burning the bacon." He dashed over, grabbed an oven mitt, and shifted the pan of blackening bacon off the burner. With a grin, he looked back at me. "There goes my breakfast." He laughed giddily, throwing up his hands. "Hell, I don't even care!" He swept over and caught me in his arms again.

More kissing. More hugging. It was getting hard to tell where Toff's body ended and mine began. "I can't believe it. I can't believe this is real," he said. "You love me. You love me, Geordi."

Yes, I loved Toff. But I wasn't *in* love with him. Even I knew there was a difference.

And I knew I could never tell Toff how I really felt—or didn't feel—about him.

Never.

CHAPTER 5

TOFF AND I lazily shot hoops in his driveway. It was the kind of thing we might do on a quiet Sunday morning in summer, so there was nothing unusual about that. Except… something was different.

Toff was so happy. The grin on his face never turned off. He was all primed and pumped up.

And how did I feel, you may wonder?

Punked.

Pixelated.

Panicked!

Don't get me wrong. I was glad to see Toff happy, and I did everything I could to hide my anxiety from him. If anybody deserved a bit of joy, it was definitely him. So why did this particular delight of his make me want to bang my head against a lamppost?

After making the rebound off my latest missed shot, Toff stopped and looked at me. For the first time, his grin dimmed. "Your game is off, man. What're you thinking about?"

I told the truth. "You."

The grin got big again. I could practically feel his bursting emotions swell across the driveway at me like a flare. He wiped sweat from his forehead with the back of his hand. "It's starting to get hot out here. Did you have breakfast?"

"No. I skipped it so I could get over here and talk to you."

"Let's walk to the deli and have some bacon biscuits. I'm buying."

He tossed the basketball into the yard and led the way toward the sidewalk. Bringing up the rear, I studied him. He'd put on a red tank top and blue jeans and his neon green kicks, which pretty much glowed against the white sidewalk. The summer sun had started putting blond streaks in his spiky brown hair. I could picture him riding waves off some California beach and breaking girls' hearts.

He looked back at me, smiling. "Come on," he urged. When I caught up to him, he reached his hand out to me.

The gesture confused my little brain. "What?"

"You had your coming out yesterday. This is my coming out." He wiggled his hand at me.

Now I got it.

Cooper-Young is the most gay-tolerant neighborhood in Memphis. Many of the shops and homes there proudly fly the rainbow flag. While you don't see a whole lot of same-sex couples holding hands in the area, that show of affection does happen from time to time. There was no reason that Toff and I walking hand in hand down the street should have made either of us uncomfortable.

I was proud of Toff, coming out on his own terms (not like me), and of course I was going to support him in this—as well as maintain the whole we're-in-love thing. I took his hand, he smiled at me, and we strolled off side by side. Scores of people were out enjoying the beautiful day, getting in their exercise or doing their shopping before the heat reached egg-frying-on-the-sidewalk levels. Nobody gave us hateful stares, spat on the ground we walked, or made the sign of the cross in our direction.

Still, holding Toff's hand gave me a weird sensation. And especially troubling was the realization that I couldn't explain to myself why I felt that way.

Walking down the street toward us, a very pretty girl, somewhere in her late teens, looked surprised when she spotted us. As we drew even with her, the surprise in her face settled into a gooey-eyed expression. "Aw," she sighed, "you guys are such a cute couple."

A cute guy couple? Where? I turned, looking over my shoulder for the adorable pair.

Toff squeezed my hand proudly.

Oh. Right.

Eek.

THE PATIO behind Paulson's Deli was shaded by a trellis covered with a thick growth of trailing ivy vines. Potted peace lilies sporting big white blooms were spaced along the outer edges. Soft, relaxing smooth jazz songs flowed gently from speakers mounted on the wall. Mom and Dad often started their date nights here. They said it was a romantic spot.

I just thought it was a cool place to grab a great sandwich.

Toff and I sat at a table in the middle of the patio having a late breakfast of bacon biscuits and orange juice. We were surrounded by couples, including but not limited to: a lesbian pair who'd moved their chairs so close together they were practically sitting in each other's laps; a grungy looking guy and gal who took turns feeding each other bites off the same tuna salad sub; and an older couple who occasionally reached across their table to hold hands while they drank coffee and ate raisin bagels.

My bacon biscuit was delicious. I'd topped the whole thing off with honey, mustard, and barbecue sauce, which made it perfect. As I ate, I watched a fair-sized bird repeatedly dive-bomb an orange, tigery-looking cat that walked along the fence line at the end of the deli's property. The feline had apparently gotten too close to the bird's nest or something. The cat was bigger, but it must not have liked all the squawking and beak jabs; after the bird's sixth dive, the cat scampered under the fence, disappearing into the alley beyond.

Grinning, I reached for my carton of orange juice and saw Toff staring at me. Like, hard. I froze, my hand hovering over the carton. Did I have bacon or something stuck between my two front teeth? I tried a quick tongue probe but didn't feel anything. "Uh... what's up?"

"Nothing," he said quietly. "It's just that I like your eyes. They're sexy."

"Oh. Thanks." I scratched my neck. It wasn't itching. "Toff?"

He leaned toward me. "Yeah, Geordi?"

How do I put this? "Are you sure... you say you've had feelings for me for a while now and—"

"A year. I've had these feelings for a year. I remember exactly when they started. It was the day after your birthday, and we were hanging at Overton Square with Jess and her friend Taylor. You were wearing those crazy jeans your mom got you, the ones with the big red lip-shaped patch on the butt that said 'kiss me.' I kept looking at that patch when you walked. I listened to you talk and laugh, and it was like I was hearing your voice, *really* hearing your voice for the first time. And it hit me." He shrugged helplessly. "I don't know how to explain it, but I got crazy attracted to you. Before you were just Geordi, my friend. You were always there, even before Jess came along, the one person who's always had my back. And now suddenly I got this big hard-on for you."

I choked on the orange juice I'd just sipped from my carton. "Sorry," I gasped, coughing. "That went down the wrong way."

"You okay?"

"Fine. I'm cool." I coughed again, finally clearing my throat. "But Toff, have you really thought about this? I mean, just because you think somebody's sexy doesn't mean you're in love with that person."

"Don't worry, Geordi, this is real." Toff reached over and caressed the back of my hand with his fingers. "I know it's real because there's this connection between us, like brothers but more than that. You understand me better than anybody else in my life. I know I love you because you mean everything to me."

"I wish you'd told me this before now."

"I wish I had too. But I didn't know you were gay, and my dad...."

"What about your dad?"

"Forget it. That doesn't matter," he said emphatically. He took my hand and squeezed it hard. "*This* is all that matters to me. Us. You and me."

I still wasn't clear on just when the "you and me" part came about.

The opening strains of the *Star Wars* theme bubbled from my pocket, disrupting both the quiet mood set by the smooth jazz and my increasingly awkward conversation with my best friend. That didn't stop me from wondering, as I pulled the cell phone from my pocket, just where my relationship with Toff was heading now. I carefully extracted my other hand from Toff's grip and held up my index finger to him in the universal "one second" sign. "Hello."

"Geordi, where are you?"

"I'm at the deli with Toff, Mom."

"Is everything okay?"

No! "Uh, yeah, everything's fine. Why?"

"You said you'd be back in an hour. That was three hours ago. It's fine. I just wanted to make sure nothing had gone wrong. Have fun with your friend, honey. Dinner's at five. See you then."

"Yeah, okay."

She hung up. I sat there with the silent phone to my ear.

"That was your mom, huh?" said Toff.

I nodded and shoved my phone back in my pocket.

"Everything okay?"

"Uh, she wants me home. Now."

Toff looked worried. "You're not in trouble or anything, are you?"

"No. No. She just wants me to do some stuff. Make up my bed—"

"You always make your bed first thing. You do that before you brush your teeth or take a shower in the morning."

"Well, I didn't make the bed today. I was… in a rush to get to your place. Yeah, that's it. And I also have to clean out my closet, clean out the garage, and clean out some other stuff."

Toff laughed. "Do I need to send your mom a copy of the child labor laws?"

I laughed too, only mine sounded totally fake. "Ha-ha. No, man. You know how my mom is about pulling my fair share around the house."

"Yeah. Let's finish our breakfast, and then I'll go home with you."

"I've got a lot to do, man. You'll be bored out of your skull at my place when you could be doing something fun."

"I just don't want to let you go right now." He leaned toward me again. "Let's go out later. You and me. It'll be our first date."

"First date. Yeah. Okay." How can you turn down someone who's looking at you with big, innocent, lonely puppy dog eyes?

"After dinner. Six o'clock. I'll come by your place. We'll play some miniature golf."

"That sounds good."

We finished our meal, discarded our trash, and started our walk home. Toff didn't hold my hand on the return trip. That turned out to be a good thing. When we started down Tanglewood Street, we spotted Jess sitting on the front steps of her house with Caitlin. They were huddled close together, talking and giggling in that secretive, intimate way only girls can pull off. Jess saw us as we passed and waved. Caitlin waved too. Their smiles seemed friendly enough, but I got the distinct impression neither of them wanted Toff and me to stop for a chat.

"Well, those two can't seem to get enough of each other," I said once we were well past the Sanchez home. "They spent most of their time at my party hanging out together."

"You know how Jess is when she makes a new friend," said Toff. "She gets really clingy sometimes. She was that way with Taylor."

"Whatever happened to that dude anyway? For a while there, he and Jess were practically dating."

"Ha. I think they were having sex."

"Maybe they just grew apart. My mom said that happens to people sometimes."

"Well, that's not gonna happen to us." He took my hand.

We rounded the corner onto Toff's street, and minutes later we were standing face-to-face on his front porch. Mr. Toffler's car was still gone.

"Thanks for breakfast, Toff."

"Thanks for walking me home, Geordi."

We stood looking at each other. In the silence that followed, something heated passed between us, a current of emotion that made me so embarrassed I turned away. Toff caught my shoulder and turned me back to him. He leaned in, closed his eyes, and kissed me softly.

"Man, I can't wait to see you again," he said.

"Yeah. Same here." If I stood there, I knew Toff would start up the kissing again, and then I might not get away at all. I needed to think over what was happening between us and try to figure a way to put things back to normal without hurting Toff. "Later, dude."

Despite the hot, humid afternoon, I headed home at a full run.

HALF A block from my house, the *Star Wars* theme started up in my pocket. I pulled out my phone. "Hello."

"What up, dude?"

The voice was completely unlike any of my friends or relatives—suave and glib. "Who is this?"

There was a quick, surprised sigh on the other end. "Damn. I think my feelings are hurt. It's Jake."

Ohmigod! Ohmigod! I stopped in my tracks. "Jake! Sorry, man. I didn't recognize your voice. How did you get my number?"

"I had my dad call your dad and get it for me. Whatcha up to?"

"I was just hanging out with a friend. I'm headed home now." Jake went out of his way to get my number. *My* number. Sweet! "What're you up to?"

"Right now I'm talking to you. I was thinking it would be cool to hang with you sometime."

Oh wow. "Hey, that would be awesome."

"Glad you think so. How about later this afternoon?"

"*This* afternoon? Oh. Sorry, I can't. I've already got something planned."

"Too bad. What're you doing tomorrow?"

"Tomorrow? Nothing. Nada." *Come take me, I'm yours!*

"My mom's driving into Memphis tomorrow for some kind of fund-raiser at the museum. What say I have her drop me by your place around noon? We can play video games or something."

"That sounds gr—" Wait, pump the brakes. My place? With Toff only a couple of blocks away? I wouldn't be doing anything wrong, just playing video games with a guy I've known for years. But I didn't feel comfortable with the idea that Toff might drop by during Jake's visit. In fact, that idea scared the bejesus out of me. "Uh… Jake? Would it be okay if I come by your place tomorrow instead?"

"Not a problem, man. Maybe I'll even do lunch for us. You still like chili cheese popcorn?"

"Love it."

"All right, then. See ya tomorrow."

"You bet."

I hung up feeling stunned. Me and Jake Butcher. Hanging out tomorrow. Heaven liked me.

DAD WAS sitting on the bench in the foyer, reading the Sunday paper, when I walked in. He always sat there when he wanted to ambush me.

"Hi, Dad."

"Hello, son." He folded the paper and put it aside. I rushed, trying to make it to the hall. He stopped me with "So. Did you hear from Jake today?"

"Yeah, I did. See you around, Dad. I think I'll watch TV in my room—"

"Pump your brakes, Geordi. I just want to have a little conversation with you." He patted the bench beside him. "Have a seat."

I rolled my eyes upward. *Seriously, God, just take me out now.* I sat down.

Dad looked at me in a way that was slyly knowing and sweetly happy at the same time. "Jake's never called you before. What did you guys talk about?"

Jeez, Dad. There is a little thing called privacy, you know. "Nothing."

"Come on. The kid didn't go out of his way to call you for nothing."

"Dad, the entire conversation lasted less than five minutes. I'm telling you, it was nothing."

"But he obviously wanted something."

Dad paused, waiting for me to spill. I didn't want to give him a single detail because he'd take whatever I said and blow it way out of proportion. I shook my head in his eager face and kept my mouth shut.

"He asked you out, didn't he?"

"What? No."

Dad gave me that shrewd look again. "He did. I know it. He wants you to go out with him."

"Jake did not ask me to go on any date. He just wants us to hang out."

"Hang out, huh?" Dad nudged his elbow into my side. "You dog you. You got your first date."

"It's not a date! We're just gonna hang out at his place tomorrow, eat popcorn, and play video games. That's it."

I didn't know it was possible for a person to actually radiate excitement until Dad did it. I could just about see the stuff shine from his pores. He lifted his face up as if to shout breaking news to every extraterrestrial in outer space. "My son's going out on his very first date. This is amazing!"

"I keep telling you, it's no date. I don't know if Jake is even gay. We're just friends hanging out. That's all."

"What time are you supposed to be at his house tomorrow?"

"Around noon." Can someone please strangle this conversation to death?

"Okay, I will drive you."

"I was gonna ask Mom to take me."

"No, I'll do it."

"Dad, you're working tomorrow."

"I'll take my lunch break and come get you."

"That doesn't make any sense. Mom's off the whole summer. She's a teacher, remember? I'll get her to drive me."

"Your mom's doing Pilates with her friends in the morning. You know how involved she gets. I'll take you. I don't want you to be late for your first date."

"It's not a freaking—!" I caught myself before my voice rose into a screech. After a long, deep breath, I sighed angrily and said, "Jeez, Dad, are you *trying* to make me do drugs? For the last time, I'm not going on a date with Jake Butcher."

"Mr. and Mrs. Butcher will both be at the museum tomorrow afternoon. Can we trust you two hormone-popping boys alone with each other?" He winked at me. Twice.

"*Arrrggghhh!*"

My voice was deeper, so this time the scream didn't sound like a girl's.

I NEEDED to talk with someone sane since I wasn't sure I qualified in that arena after my chat with Dad. Finally shut away in my room, I pulled out my phone and dialed Jessica.

After four rings, her voicemail picked up. She'd recorded a new greeting. "Hi, you got Jess, but I'm not taking calls right now. Please leave a message telling me what you want, and if I give a damn about it, I'll call you back. Peace."

I didn't leave a message.

CHAPTER 6

A GUY'S first date is important. I wanted to make sure Toff's was special.

After dinner—zucchini lasagna with soy cheese, and yes, it tastes about as good as it sounds—I walked to a gift shop and spent the eight bucks I had left after the movie the other day. Back home, I showered and dressed in fresh jeans and a clean T-shirt. At 5:45, I told Mom and Dad I was going to the arcade to play miniature golf with Toff and left. A few minutes later, I arrived at the Toffler home and rang the bell.

Mr. Toffler's car was still gone.

Toff opened the door, looking happily surprised. "Hey. I said I'd pick *you* up."

"I figured I'd do the honors." I was struck by Toff's appearance. He wore a new polo shirt that accented his fine shoulders and chest. His loose jeans were starched, and he wore new kicks so white they almost shone. He'd tamed his short, flyaway hair by combing it back and slicking it to his scalp. That had the effect of highlighting the sculpted angles of his cheekbones and jawline. His soft smile and greenish brown eyes were filled with pleasure. I'd never seen him this alive, this freaking beautiful. "Dag. You look amazing."

"So do you."

He was wearing cologne, the first time I'd ever known him to do such a thing. The scent was breezy and light, like ocean air. I'd never been to the ocean, but that's what the cologne made me think of. I could see Toff in swim trunks, standing on a beach, the sun washing over his tight bare skin—"Well! Are you ready?"

"Yeah, sure." He stepped onto the porch and locked the door behind him. "Let's go."

"Before we head for the arcade, I've got a little something to mark the occasion." I produced the present I'd been hiding behind my back. The dude at the gift shop had done a great job with the wrapping and bow.

Again Toff looked surprised. "You got me a gift?"

"Go ahead and open it."

He tore off the wrapping and lifted the lid off the small box. "A book?"

"It's a memory book." I lifted the little book and held it up for Toff to get a closer look. On the front was "My First Date," and below that was a picture frame built right into the front cover. "You can use it to keep pictures and mementos and stuff about our date today."

Toff took the memory book and stared at me, his eyes filling with affection. It was disconcerting, having him look at me as if the world would end if I weren't in it. "This is great, Geordi. Thanks."

"Come here. We can start working on the book right now." I looped my arm around Toff's neck, pulled him close, and held out my cell phone in front of us for a selfie. "Smile, dude."

He held the book up to his chest and grinned like there was no tomorrow.

I took several shots with us in different poses, ending with one of Toff kissing me on the cheek.

We looked at the pictures before leaving for the arcade. I had to admit, Toff and I looked good together. We really would have made a cute couple if we… if I, that is, was actually in… you know.

WE PLAYED two rounds of miniature golf. Afterward we shared a banana split at Otherlands Coffee Bar. I don't remember a lot of the details. There was music, both at the arcade and the coffee bar. We talked a bit—about what, I couldn't tell you. I think Toff was too happy for conversation. And I was happy he was happy.

I do remember taking more selfies for the memory book. Toff took some too. But mostly I remember us holding hands across the table as we ate.

Holding hands with him still felt strange.

AT TOFF'S house I went straight to his room and threw myself on the bed, like always.

Annnd… that was probably not the wisest thing to do under the circumstances.

I jumped up and stood at attention as Toff walked in. "You want a Pepsi or something?" he asked.

"No, I'm cool."

Toff liked to get comfortable once he was home. The first thing he did when he made it in from school was to trade out his uniform for something loose and light. Standing barely three feet away from me, he kicked off his sneakers at once. He proceeded to pull his polo shirt over his head and toss it aside. He wasn't wearing anything underneath it. Then he unbuckled his jeans.

Oh, God, please *let him have on drawers!*

Off came the jeans, revealing a pair of striped boxers. Hm. When did he trade in his tighty-whities for boxers? And when did he get all those muscles in his legs? Lean, hard muscles that flexed so magnificently when he—Oh look, there's a Godzilla poster on the wall over his desk. Isn't that interesting? I've only seen it like, a thousand times.

"Geordi, hand me that shirt over there."

I grabbed the tank top he'd left draped over the headboard of his bed and turned back to him as he pulled on a pair of basketball shorts. He slipped into the tank top. His hair had started sticking up in spots again. I reached out impulsively and vigorously mussed his hair with both hands.

He laughed. "What're you doing?"

I stood back, looking him over with his hair spiked in all its glory. "I like you this way."

He stepped in and kissed me. "Mm. You taste like strawberry ice cream."

"So do you."

"I'm thirsty. I'm gonna have some water. You sure you don't want anything?"

"Now that you mention it, I'll have some water. With lots of ice."

"You got it."

Toff left for the kitchen, and I ambled over to his desk. Sketch pads of various sizes were stacked at one side of the desk. Several pencils—color, charcoal, and regular old graphite—were scattered across the desktop. Toff was an artist. He'd been drawing since he was old enough to sit up and put a pencil to paper. When we were in elementary school, he drew a lot of comics that were funny as hell and got passed around, keeping me, Jess, and many of our little friends entertained. Now he did mostly still-life drawings.

He'd labeled each of the pads with the dates he started and finished sketching in them. The pad on top was the most recent, with a start date of March of this year and no end date yet. I picked it up and began flipping through it.

First was a picture of the main entrance of our school. Next was a picture of an old, unlaced work boot, then a mailbox mounted on a post in the middle of grassy field. A wine glass lying broken on a table, a car on an empty road with its driver's door open, a teddy bear sitting in a chair with its eyes torn out—my chest grew heavy with emotion as I looked at them. Toff had managed to infuse each drawing with a misty sense of melancholy, of loneliness. His talent amazed me.

The still lifes gave way to drawings of guys. Naked guys. Toff had drawn plenty of cartoon people, caricatures like the ones you see in comic strips, but this was on a totally different level. These drawings were realistic. Anatomically correct. Practically three dimensional. The guys in the pictures were of all races, some young, some older, tall, short, lean, thick. Each face bore an expression of aching solitude.

And then there was… me?

Oh, shit. There was a drawing of me in the sketch pad. Naked like the other guys. I was standing on a grassy expanse near a row of towering hedges. There was darkness in the background but a light seemed to be shining on me. Drawn in side view, my body looked about like it did in real life—which is to say my arms and legs were firm and strong from playing sports but a bit on the thin side, my pecs were just okay, my ass was small, and my junk was average. My face was turned toward the viewer. Unlike the faces in the other naked dude drawings, my expression was one of surprise.

My first reaction was pure embarrassment. It felt as if I'd just seen an actual photograph of myself sans clothing. I also felt bewildered. Why did Toff draw me that way? There was nothing about the drawing that creeped me out; in a way, it was flattering. When somebody pictures you in your birthday suit, it means you're hot, right? But then, the guys in the other drawings looked great, all rugged and handsome and seriously adult. In my drawing, I came off as some chump teen dork who'd for sure be easier on the eyes dressed than undressed. I mean, really, what the hell was I in there for? Was Toff going to stick a caption above my picture that said, "Don't let this happen to you"?

"What do you think?"

I jerked so hard the pad flew out of my hand. "Dag, Toff! You scared the crap out of me."

He smiled. "Sorry, man. Here, have some water." He handed me a glass and then reached down to retrieve the sketch pad.

"You're really good, dude. You're doing some serious art now."

"I've always been serious about my art."

"No, I mean you've got real talent. You can actually put feelings into your stuff."

"That's what art's all about. Putting feelings into the stroke of a pen or a brush."

"Well, you should major in art when you get to college. Going for anything else would just be a waste. In my opinion. For what that's worth."

Toff drank some water and put his glass on the desk. Then he opened the sketch pad again to the drawing of yours truly. "I was worried this would creep you out when you saw it."

I shrugged. "No, nothing like that. But... why did you draw me that way?"

"I drew it right after I left your coming-out party. I couldn't stop thinking about you, about how much you turn me on. And then I remembered that pool party your dad threw for your twelfth birthday. That was the only time I've actually seen you naked—"

"Jeez!" I growled, letting my head fall back. "I thought that was dead and buried."

"You thought wrong." Toff patted me sympathetically on the shoulder. "Anyway, I'm doing nudes now. And remembering that incident at the pool party sort of inspired me."

"But why draw me naked when my body is so freaky-looking?"

"Come on, Geordi. You're not freaky-looking. You have a nice body."

"I have a nice face. My body's a different story."

"You're hot. Take off your clothes and I'll prove it to you."

I shoved him away with my shoulder, he shoved me back, and we both laughed. And for that brief moment, things were normal between us again.

WE PRINTED the pictures of our date from our cell phones and Toff put them in his memory book, along with the ticket stubs from our golf game and the cash register receipt from our visit to Otherlands. After that, we started a game of *Street Fighter*.

The sun had set and the windows in Toff's room were starting to grow dark. As we played, I glanced at the clock on his nightstand: 8:29. Mr. Toffler hadn't come home yet.

"Have you talked to your dad, man?"

Toff didn't take his eyes off the television screen. "No. I sent him a couple of texts. He hasn't texted me back." His hands visibly tightened on the controls, a stranglehold that was a sure sign his mood had just taken a deep dive.

I didn't ask any more questions about his dad.

FIFTEEN MINUTES later, Toff suddenly switched off the game console.

"We're through playing?" I asked, surprised.

"Yeah. Now I wanna play with you."

Uh-oh.

He stood up, took my hand, and pulled me to my feet. For a few moments, he let his eyes roam all over my face as if trying to memorize what I looked like. His eyes closing, he slowly moved in, slipped his arms around my shoulders, and kissed me. He kissed me again and again.

As the minutes ticked off, his kisses went from tender to aggressive, and my level of discomfort shot up like a bottle rocket on the Fourth of July. It wasn't that I didn't like the kisses, per se. I'm totally and exclusively into guys. Toff is a guy, and he's cute. What totally and exclusively gay teenage dude wouldn't like kissing a cute guy? But I felt as if I'd been caught in a trap that was steadily tightening around me.

Okay, don't panic. You can do this. Just go with the flow. I had my arms around Toff's waist, and I was kissing him back. I closed my eyes and settled into the action. When Toff slipped his tongue into my mouth, I barely flinched. *It's good. It's all good.*

Slowly, he moved his arms from my shoulders. I felt his hands slip onto my back. His fingers dug into my lats, massaging deeply. It felt pretty damn good. After a few minutes of that, he moved his hands down... and down....

My eyes flew open.

I pulled my head back, breaking the kiss. It felt as if I'd plunged deep into some crazy alternate universe, as if rain had started falling up from the floor right there in the room. I was horrified. "Are you... feeling my ass?"

Toff's eyes were closed seventh heaven style. "Oh *hell* yeah," he growled. Then he seemed to register my discomfort. He opened his eyes and gave me a worried, questioning look. "What? Am I doing it wrong or something?"

"No. You definitely seem to have the hang of it."

He took one hand off my butt long enough to grab the back of my head and pull me into the kiss again, and then he returned his hand down south. He pressed himself roughly against my thigh, and that's when I felt his—uh, shall we say—"enthusiasm."

Please, a little help here, God, Allah, Yahweh… Satan. Somebody!

Toff fell back on his bed, pulling me down with him. His tongue seemed to have lodged halfway down my throat, swabbing my tonsils.

Okay, it was definitely time to put a stop to this.

I pushed him away with both hands. "Toff…. Toff, wait. Wait a second."

He opened his eyes and looked at me as if I'd cut off his air supply. "What? What's wrong?"

"Don't you think this is going too fast?"

"No, not fast enough." He eagerly reached for me again.

I pressed him back to the mattress. "Stop. Slow your roll, man."

He squinted at me, confused. "Geordi?"

"What if your dad comes back and catches us?"

"Don't worry. He won't." Toff lunged up to kiss me again.

I pulled away. "What do you mean?"

"My dad does this all the time. He'll take off somewhere for hours and hours and won't answer my calls. He's not coming back, not anytime soon, probably not until sometime tomorrow."

"Dag. That's messed-up."

"Yeah, well it is what it is."

As before, mention of Mr. Toffler took Toff's mood down. Still holding me by the waist, he lay back on the bed, looking tired suddenly.

Could this situation get any more awkward? "It's after nine. I should get home."

"Yeah…." He let me go, rolled away, and sat on the edge of the bed.

I stood up and straightened my clothes. I held out my hand to him. "Come on, walk me to the door."

He took my hand and led me to the living room. At the front door, we stopped. Toff kissed me, just a peck on the lips. "Thanks for going out with me, Geordi," he said with the tiniest of smiles, "and for the memory book. I won't ever forget this."

"I had fun with you tonight, Toff." And that was true.

We looked at each other. Toff seemed so small. Afraid. Broken and thrown away. Out of the blue, I grabbed him in a tight hug. I didn't want him to be alone. "Come to my house," I whispered at his ear. "Spend the night."

"Do you, do you think that would be okay with your mom and dad?"

He'd spent the night with me dozens of times while we were growing up. This wouldn't be any different. I let him go, stepped back, took out my cell phone, and dialed home.

"Hello."

"Hi, Mom. I'm at Toff's. His dad had to go out of town and won't be back until tomorrow. Is it okay if Toff spends the night at our house?"

"Of course, honey. You know your friends are always welcome."

"Okay, thanks. Toff's gonna grab a change of clothes and we'll be there in a few minutes."

"Fine. We'll see you guys then."

As I disconnected the call, I gave Toff a thumbs-up. "It's all set, man. Let's get outta here."

He beamed at me.

BY THE time we made it to my house, Dad had already dug out and inflated the air mattress, and Mom had it on the floor of my bedroom, all made up with fresh linen.

"Thanks for letting me sleep over, Mr. and Mrs. Quintrell," Toff said.

"We're always glad to have you, Toff," said Dad. "It's nice to have someone around to keep ol' Geordi here entertained."

"Yeah, and I really like playing with ol' Geordi." He winked at me. I choked.

"Are you okay, honey?" Mom patted me on the back.

"Yeah. That just went down the wrong way."

"But... you aren't drinking anything."

And yet it felt as if I were drowning. "Toff and I are gonna watch a movie before we go to sleep."

"Something loud and full of explosions, no doubt," Dad said. "Well, keep your door shut so you guys don't disturb your mom and me."

Toff saluted. "Will do, Mr. Quintrell."

Mom gave Toff a frown. She stared intensely at him for a few moments as if studying his face. "Toff, come here," she said, waving him toward her.

Toff walked over to Mom. She wrapped her arms around him, hugging him warmly for what seemed a long time. When she let him go, Toff's face had a puzzled expression. "What was that for?" he asked.

"You just look as if you needed it." Mom patted his cheek tenderly. "Go. Go watch your obnoxious movie."

Mom and Dad headed for the living room. I closed my bedroom door, and Toff tossed the backpack with his clothes, toothpaste, and toothbrush into the corner by the air mattress. I walked over to my bed, grabbed the remote control, turned on the television, and pulled up the menu of movies currently available for streaming. "What do you wanna watch?"

"How about *Justice League vs. Teen Titans*?" said Toff. He hopped in my bed and pushed his back up against the headboard. "I haven't seen that one in a while."

"Cool." I punched up the movie and settled in the bed next to Toff.

The movie started. We watched for a while, saying nothing.

"You didn't tell your mom and dad, did you?" Toff asked abruptly without taking his eyes off the screen.

"Tell them what?"

"That I'm gay and that we're dating."

"Uh, no, I didn't."

"I figured that. Otherwise I don't think they would've been too keen on the two of us sleeping together in your room with the door closed."

"Just to be clear, we're not sleeping together. You're sleeping down there on the air mattress, and I'm sleeping up here on my bed."

"Okay, I get it. We're not rushing into anything. I can do with kisses." He flicked a devious smile in my direction. "For now."

I got a chill when he said that. I couldn't tell if it was a good chill or a bad chill.

We fell silent for another while, watching the buildup for the title showdown between the Titans and the Justice League. We both laughed at the scene where shape-changing Beast Boy morphed back to his human form naked in front of Raven.

"You're gonna tell 'em, right?" Toff asked. "About you and me."

"You and me. Yeah. Lots to talk about there. I'll get around to it." I reached over and patted his knee. "Now let's shut up and watch the movie, okay?"

CHAPTER 7

MONDAY MORNING, Toff and I slept in. By the time we finally crawled out of bed, Dad was at work and Mom was off to the gym for Pilates. We ate a breakfast of Pop-Tarts—which Toff brought from his own kitchen because he knew what he'd find in mine—and then we got into our swim trunks, went into the backyard, grabbed the hose, and started filling plastic bazookas for a water gun fight.

While we were loading up, I casually said, "I have to get you back home about 11:00 this morning, Toff. I promised a friend I'd hang out with him at his place today."

"Yeah? What friend?"

"Jake Butcher. You never met him."

"Oh, you mentioned him before. He's the son of your dad's boss."

"That's him. We've known each other all these years, but we've never really gotten together outside of functions at the Pink Palace. We decided it's time to change that." I watched Toff's eyes carefully as I spoke; he showed no sign of being upset.

"That sounds good. While you're at Jake's, maybe I'll hang out with Jess or Carson."

"Carson? As in Meyer?"

"Come on, Geordi. Carson's not that bad. He's kinda cool actually. And you must think so too or he wouldn't have been at your party the other day."

"My dad invited him, not me."

"Whatever. Hey, Geordi."

"Yeah?"

"Suck on this!" He hit me dead in the face with a blast from his bazooka.

Water shot up my nose so hard and fast I was sure it went straight through my sinuses and spewed out my ears. I fell back, snorting like a drowned hog and laughing at the same time. Once my nose was clear, I looked at my friend with water dripping from my head and play murder in my eyes.

"Toff, you are *so* dead."

"Promises, promises," he quipped as he fired off another blast.

The fight went on for about an hour. We were both soaked by the time I called an end to the festivities. We went inside, showered (separately), got dressed, and I walked Toff home. Mr. Toffler's car wasn't parked in the driveway when we arrived.

I hated to bring up the subject, but I needed to know. "Have you heard from your dad, Toff?"

"I called him while you were in the shower," Toff said matter-of-factly. "It went straight to voicemail. I left a message."

"Did he ever call you back?"

Toff pulled out his phone and checked. "Nope."

Before we left Toff's place last night, I asked him if he was going to leave a note for his father in case the man came back, and Toff said no. Mr. Toffler was a construction worker with Magnum Home Builders. It was possible he came home late last night or this morning to no Toff and no clue as to where Toff was. Now he'd gone off to work, and the man didn't even make a phone call to see if his son was alive and well. I didn't understand Mr. Toffler. I did not understand him at all.

Standing on his porch, Toff slipped his backpack off his shoulder and turned to me. "Okay. I guess I'll see you later."

I took Toff by the arm and instinctively pushed him against the wall next to the front door, away from the windows where the absent Mr. Toffler couldn't see us if he'd been there to look outside. "Yeah, I'll call you when I get home." And then I planted a kiss on his mouth.

What the heck? It felt like the right thing to do at the moment.

I AM not attracted to Jake Butcher.

I am not attracted to handsome Jake Butcher.

I am not attracted to hot damn handsome Jake Butcher.

I am not attracted to hell hot damn handsome and oh-so-fine Jake Butch—

"What's that, Geordi?" said Dad, flicking a look over at me as he drove. "What did you say?"

I felt the heat creep across my face. "Huh?" I said, stalling until I could dream up an actual answer.

"You were mumbling just now. What have your mother and I always told you, son? Don't mumble. Speak up! Your voice is important, and you should make yourself heard. What were you trying to say just now? Something about hell and hot and Jake Butcher?"

Oh jeez. "Uhm… er… hey, Dad, when you pick me up this afternoon, can we stop by Sears so I can get some boxers? I'm kinda tired of wearing the tighty-whities."

"Ah. My little buddy is growing up. He's ready to hang loose like a man." Dad sniffed and wiped a fake tear from his eye. "Another threshold crossed. I'm so happy for you, son." He sighed dramatically.

"Yeah, thanks, just drive, Dad, please."

Even with the relatively light midday traffic, it was going to take a bit more than thirty minutes to reach Arlington. That was like a lifetime when I was riding alone with Dad.

"So. Obviously you were thinking about Jake just now," Dad said.

"T-shirts. Maybe I should get some new T-shirts too when we shop for the boxers. A lot of the ones I have now have gotten really stretchy. And some of them have got holes right in the armpit. What good's a T-shirt with a hole in the armpit?"

"You must really like Jake, huh? Tell me—"

"Socks! You should get me some more absorbent socks. I notice my sneakers are starting to stink when I take them off. I can't go around with stinky feet, Dad. It might get a little awkward if I'm over at Jess's and kick off my shoes and everybody in the house passes out."

"Geordi, why don't we stick with one topic of conversation here? You don't have to be ashamed of having feelings for Jake. It's perfectly natural for you to have them."

"Dad, I don't have feelings for Jake. I just like him as a friend."

"Always be honest with yourself, son. No good comes from holding back and hiding things. That's no way to live your life. Your mom and I want you to be happy."

"I am happy, Dad. And you know what would make me even happier right now?"

"What's that?"

"If we could talk about stinky feet. As in, how do I get rid of them? Not the feet, I want to keep those. They kinda come in handy… or feety… sometimes. I just want to get rid of the stink."

Dad sighed. That one was a genuine sigh. "Okay, son. Let's talk stinky feet."

THE BUTCHER house was bigger and a lot newer than the one I lived in.

Mom talked a lot about carbon footprints. She said you can't leave small ones living in a big-ass house. When Dad got promoted to director at the museum and started picking up a much larger paycheck, he floated the idea of looking for a bigger house, maybe in Harbor Town on the river. Mom shot that down real quick, saying the modest-sized bungalow we'd lived in since I was born was perfect for us. He practically had to beg to get the pool and landscaping lights installed because Mom said they would just add to the already staggering amount of soot humanity was pumping into the atmosphere.

Yeah, maybe we could survive just fine in a not-so-big house without a pool or landscaping lights, and I worried about how humans were trashing the earth as much as Mom did. But there was a lot I liked about Jake's house. For starters, it had a large, kidney-shaped, in-ground pool that put the one in my backyard to shame. Also, it had a "media room" with overstuffed recliners and a wall-mounted television sporting a screen seven feet wide. And there was a popcorn machine in the corner exactly like the ones in movie theaters.

But best of all, it had Jake. And maybe that's why I overlooked all the excesses at the Butcher house that would have driven Mom right up a wall.

"What up, Geordi?" he said coolly when he opened the front door to me. Then he waved over my shoulder and called out, "Hey, Mr. Quintrell."

Dad waved back, smiling as he drove off.

"So you made it. Come on in." Jake stepped aside to let me in and shut the door after me. "I was watching a movie. I've got the popcorn machine loaded and ready to go, and the chili's on the stove. This way."

I would have followed him anywhere. Probably right off a cliff. He was wearing tight cut-off-at-the-knee blue jeans. His butt looked fantastic in those cutoffs. Yes, I was staring.

That's why I tripped on the rug. "Ulp!" I gasped as I went down on one knee.

Jake came back to me. "Hey, you okay, man?"

"Yeah, I'm all right. I guess I just didn't see that rug." The rug was around six feet square and bright yellow. Kind of hard to miss, actually.

As he helped me to my feet, I looked through the window and spotted the pool past the patio. The blue water sparkled in the sunlight. I loved pools and I loved swimming. Sometimes I think I should have been born a fish.

Jake must have noticed my interest. "You want to take a dip?"

"I didn't bring my trunks."

"You can borrow a pair of mine."

"Well… maybe later."

"There's no time like the present." He gave me a crooked grin.

It was too cute to resist. "Okay."

He took me upstairs to his room. As he went to his dresser, I noticed the guitar leaning against the footboard of his bed. "Oh. Do you play guitar?" I asked. I wasn't usually so easily distracted, but thoughts of Toff had popped into my head, and I was trying very hard not to focus on Jake's body.

"I fool around on it some," he replied. "My mom got me that for Christmas when I was ten. Said I had an aptitude for music. That thing sat in my closet for over a year before I finally picked it up."

"Well, was she right?"

He paused as if considering his answer. "You be the judge."

Jake sauntered over, picked up the guitar, and sat on the end of the bed. He began to pluck at the strings, sending a riff of notes sprinkling through the air that I instantly recognized as the opening of "Twinkle Twinkle Little Star." He smiled slyly as if he'd just made a joke, and I was hypnotized by the dimples in his cheeks. Then I was mesmerized by his flexing biceps. After giving myself a mental slap across the face, I turned and looked around the room.

No posters decorated the walls, just two big elegantly framed photographs of motorcycles, which was probably Mrs. Butcher's idea as to what kind of ornamentation suited a teenage guy's room. A big bulletin board was mounted over the headboard of the bed sporting pictures of musicians, each playing an acoustic guitar. I didn't know who any of them were. There were also pictures of guitars that had apparently been cut out of a catalog. A bookcase next to the desk was lined with trophies and awards, some for baseball, some for swimming, and some for science fairs. A widescreen television stood atop an entertainment center across from the bed, and below it were carefully stacked video game cartridges and a game console.

A shift in the music drew my attention back to Jake. His eyes were closed and he was bobbing his head slightly as his fingers flew up and down, back and forth, over the strings and struts. He was smiling big, and I could hear why. The music he strummed out was bright, airy, a bouncy tune so playful it filled me with joy and made me want to dance. My head weaved side to side with the beat as if the music had taken complete control. The song flowed over me for several minutes, steadily sweeping me up in happiness. When Jake ended things on a final, dramatic stroke, I was so thrilled I broke into applause.

"Dude! That was fantastic!"

Jake bowed over his guitar. "Thanks, man."

"How do you do that, get your fingers to move so fast? I could never play guitar like that."

"Sure you could, Geordi. All it takes is practice."

"For you, maybe. I don't have any talent at all when it comes to music. I can't even sing."

"I don't believe that."

"Man, back in the spring, I was sitting in my backyard listening to some of my dad's old school R & B on my headphones. I started singing along, and my next-door neighbor called 911."

He chuckled. "Yeah, right."

"Seriously. She thought somebody was strangling cats in her backyard." He laughed out loud that time, which was more music to my ears, and I smiled at him. "What song was that you were playing?"

Jake shrugged as he began strumming random notes from the strings. "I haven't come up with a title for it yet."

"You *wrote* that?"

"Yeah," he answered casually. "I write a lot of songs."

I found myself admiring his talent, just as I admired Toff's artistic abilities. I always admired people who were capable of things I couldn't do myself in a million years. "You put a lot of life into that one," I said. "I could see blue birds flying and kids playing and sun shining the whole time you were playing. That was real feel-good music."

"Yeah. When it comes to music, a lot depends on the mood I'm in. Some of the happiest songs I've written were done when I was feeling low, when I wanted to lift myself up. Sometimes when crazy shit happens, all you can do is sing."

"Or scream."

He laughed again. "Whatever works for you."

"So you sing too?"

"Occasionally, when the mood hits. And the neighbors haven't called the police on me yet, so I guess I do all right."

I suddenly pictured myself being serenaded by this guy. "When do I get to hear you belt one out?"

"Another time." He put the guitar aside and stood up. "Right now we're going for a swim."

He went to his dresser, tugged open a drawer, and produced a pair of white trunks, which he tossed to me. He tossed a red pair, identical to the ones he'd given me except for the color, on the bed and began to undress, pulling his T-shirt over his head. When he unbuttoned his jeans, I thought I was going to start drooling.

"Uh, is it okay if I change in the bathroom or something?" I asked quickly.

"Sure. Bathroom's right there," he answered, pointing.

I hurried to the adjoining bathroom. Behind me, I heard his jeans drop on the floor. *Don't turn around. Don't turn around, you idiot. You'll turn into a pillar of salt if you turn around.*

I shut the bathroom door without giving in to temptation. And it was just about the most difficult thing I'd ever done.

WE SWAM races against each other, floated leisurely on our backs, tossed a handful of dimes in the water and went on a deep-sea treasure hunt. When we finally climbed out of the pool, we slumped in a pair of chaise lounges beneath a towering, stately magnolia tree. Children laughed in the distance. The next-door neighbor's sprinklers filled the air with a soothing swish. A strong, warm breeze blew across the yard. I felt wonderful, pleasantly tired and completely at ease.

"You having a good time, Geordi?"

"I'm wishing I didn't have to go home. What does that tell you?"

Jake didn't smile. He turned away from me, looking a bit uncomfortable, which was ironic in that just seconds ago he seemed to be worried that I wasn't all that relaxed around him. Maybe it was ducking into the bathroom before taking off my clothes that left him with that impression. I tried to think of something funny or profound to say, to put him at ease, but my mind remained stubbornly blank.

I resorted to a tried and true standard in such situations. "Hey."

"What?" said Jake, staring up at the white blossoms swaying in the breeze over our heads.

"Nothing. Just 'hey.'" *Stupid, Geordi. You sound stupid. Ugh!* "I was just trying to start a conversation."

He shrugged in response. What the hell was going on here? Only a minute ago, we were having such a good time. Now everything was just weird.

"Geordi... can I ask you something?"

"Sure, Jake."

"How long have you been gay?"

"I don't know. My mom says gay people are born this way. But I got attracted to guys around the time I was twelve." I studied his face. He was still looking up into the tree, avoiding eye contact with me. "Why do you ask?"

He shrugged again, looking even more embarrassed. "I wonder about myself sometimes."

"Wonder what?"

"If I might be gay." He sighed and closed his eyes. "I like girls. I think they're hot, and I've done my share of fooling around with a couple of them. But sometimes... sometimes I get this thing where I kinda want to... kiss a guy."

"Sometimes when? I mean, does this urge just come out of the blue or what?"

"I guess it started as a crush, more or less. Last year this dude named Ricky Spencer moved into the neighborhood, in that big gray brick house two doors down from me. He fell in with me and some of the other guys I hang with. Nice fella and all. I like him. And then, after a couple of months, I realized that I *really* like him." He turned to me, his expression uneasy. "You know what I mean?"

"I think I do. I've felt that way before."

"Well, I haven't. It's hard to be friends with Ricky now because I feel so... off when I'm around him. I want to see what it's like to kiss him and touch him. And what kinda sense does that make when I still like girls?"

He waited, looking at me as if he expected a completely logical, totally expert answer to come spilling out of my mouth. I was still hoping somebody would pop up and tell me what to do about Toff, so what could I say to Jake? "I don't know what to tell you, man."

"I don't know either," he said with a tiny sigh. "I don't think Ricky is gay. All he talks about is girls. Nobody would think I'm gay either, because all I talk about is girls too. But there's this… I guess, bi part of me, sometimes, that wants to do something with another dude…."

I got a tingle in my groin that made me want to squirm. "Like what?"

"What I said before… kiss and touch. I didn't know another guy anywhere who had feelings like that. Then, a couple of weeks ago, my dad told me your dad had called and said you had come out of the closet and there was going to be this big coming-out party to celebrate. I was totally surprised."

"You weren't the only one," I said drily.

"I have to say, I admire you. That was really bold of you, man, coming out to your family and all your friends."

"Don't admire me too much. It was more like I came out to my parents, and then they outed me to everybody else."

"Your parents are cool with it, then. You being gay."

"They threw me a fick-facking, hello-world-I'm-queer party, Jake. So yeah, I'd say it's a safe bet that they're happy with my thing for boys." A moment later his true concern dawned on me. "You think your parents won't accept it if you're gay?"

"They wouldn't kick me out of the house or anything. I don't think it would bother my mom too much. But I know my dad will be disappointed, if I'm gay or bi or something other than straight." He twisted his mouth as if that thought left a bad taste. "So have you ever actually kissed a guy?"

"A few times, yeah."

"What's it like?"

Scary as hell. "I enjoyed it well enough, but it was a little… no, it was fine. It was good."

"That's what it all comes down to for me. I won't know if I like it or not until I actually try it. When I thought about things, Geordi, after I knew you were gay, it hit me how good-looking you are. And I started wondering if maybe you'd kiss me."

"Is that why you wanted to hang out with me? So you can experiment at the whole gay thing?" *Make me your lab rat, dammit.* Please *make me your lab rat!*

"No. I wanted to hang with you because I also realized that I actually like you and I thought we could be friends, real friends. We don't have to kiss… but I think I'd really like to. If you want to, that is."

"Jake, to be honest, a year ago nobody could have paid me enough money to kiss you."

He looked shocked for a moment and then barked out a laugh. "Way to make a dude feel good about himself, man. Damn!"

"That was then. When I saw you at my party, you looked so freaking good to me I wanted to do a lot more than just kiss."

"Well, I want to start with a kiss and then see where it goes from there. So, I'm game if you're game."

Was I game? We were alone in a beautiful, relaxing setting. Jake was lying barely an arm's length away from me, his naked brown torso smooth and wet, his smoky-eyed handsome face turned toward me, his lips looking as plump and inviting as a good ol' ripe southern peach. Hell yes I wanted to kiss him! I wanted to drape myself over his muscular body like a blanket and tongue him down until it drove us both insane. He was willing to give me that and maybe even more. The situation couldn't have been more perfect if I'd ordered it off an à la carte menu.

But I kept thinking of Toff.

"I'm kinda seeing someone, Jake. I don't want to hurt him. If I kiss you and he finds out, I'm afraid that's exactly what I'll do."

"Oh." He seemed surprised and maybe just a tiny bit disappointed. "Well, I can understand that, and I'm glad you found somebody you like. Okay. Yeah. Hey, you ready for another swim?"

He smiled, friendly as ever, and bounced to his feet. I focused on the way his wet trunks clung to his magnificent butt and legs as he made a dash for the pool.

The anger and resentment hit me from nowhere, a slow, ugly, malignant burn in my head.

Across the deck, Jake sat down at the edge of the pool and slipped into the water. He went completely under and swam out a short distance. He broke through the surface in an explosive spray, the droplets of water glittering in the sunlight. As he wiped his face clear with both hands, he swiveled around and looked back at me.

"Come on," he said and laughed in that wonderfully masculine voice of his. "What're you waiting for, man? Get your ass in the water!"

I put on a smile that I didn't feel anywhere but on my lips and got up to join him.

CHAPTER 8

I WAS pissed.

"You're awfully quiet," Dad observed as he drove us home.

That's because I'm mad as hell, and it's all your *freaking fault.*

"How was your afternoon with Jake?"

"It was okay."

Dad paused. "Did something bad happen while you were there?"

"No."

"Then what's wrong?"

What was wrong was that I didn't kiss Jake when I had the chance, and now I couldn't stop kicking myself for it. "Nothing's wrong." Of course, I wouldn't have been kicking myself if Dad hadn't thrown that stupid coming-out party.

"I can tell when you're upset, son. It might help things if you talked them out with me."

"I don't want to talk." Not to you, anyway. I reached down and turned up the radio.

AT MY request Dad dropped me off at Toff's. He and I really needed to talk.

I rang the bell. Again and again.

"Hang on!" Toff called from within. He opened the door a moment later and broke into a glad smile. "Hey, Geordi. You're back, huh?"

"Hi, Toff," I greeted him quickly as I stepped past him into the house. "There's something I need to say to you." I was all set to tell him that this whole relationship thing between us was just moving too fast for me. He needed to know that I wanted us to take a step back, take a little break from each other, give ourselves time to catch our breath, and then see where our feelings actually were. I was going to say all those things, probably in a tumble of words so rushed Toff wouldn't understand any of it—until I looked over my shoulder and noticed we weren't alone.

Carson, Jessica, and Caitlin were sitting in a semicircle on the floor, holding spreads of Uno cards in their hands with a deck and scattered cards set out among them. Toff had his own cards tucked neatly in his hand. They were all looking expectantly at me.

"Say what?" Toff asked as he closed the door and moved in to face me.

"What?" I echoed, feeling distracted as I turned my gaze back to Toff.

Toff smiled, amused. "You said you had something to say."

"Oh. Well… I just wanted to know if you ever got in touch with your dad."

"I called his job. His boss told me he didn't come in today."

That news alarmed me. I started to say as much, but Toff cut me off with "Everybody's been waiting for you to get here."

"Come on over and join the game, man," Carson called to me. "I'm killing these fools at Uno."

"Yes, you're killing us all right," said Caitlin with a wicked grin. "That swollen head of yours is sucking all the oxygen out of the room."

"Good one, girl. Gimme some." Jess held up her right hand, and Caitlin high-fived her.

Fifteen-year-old Caitlin was a lot flashier than Jess. Jess wore white jeans and a light blue halter top. Her dark, shiny hair, parted simply down the middle, hung loosely over her shoulders. She never put on makeup, which she didn't really need anyway because she's naturally pretty. Caitlin wore a glittery beaded purple skirt and a tight red blouse that forced her big boobs up and out in a way that screamed, "Look at these ta-tas!" Since my coming-out party, she'd dyed her bangs neon pink. The rest of her hair retained its natural blonde color. It was pulled back in a ponytail that had been teased into such frizziness it looked as if a yellow squirrel had latched on to her scalp and gotten electrocuted. Although she was as pretty as Jess, she had painted her lips a shiny deep red and had put some kind of bright red stuff around her eyes. Every time she blinked, it was as if I were looking at a pair of flashing red lights. I'd never met Caitlin's mom, but I didn't believe for one second the woman knew her daughter had left the house with that gunk on her face.

"Okay, Toff, Geordi is here now," Jess said. "What's this big announcement you want to make about you two?"

A chill went down my back. That one was definitely unpleasant.

Toff stood up straight like an actor at the Academy Awards about to make an acceptance speech. "First of all, everybody," he said with overcooked formality, "I'm glad to have you all here. This is a very important moment in my life, and there is nobody else I'd rather share this with—"

"Man, would you just say it already?" Carson sniped impatiently. "You're taking so long I'm growing gray hair here."

"Screw you, Carson. I'm having my moment. This announcement comes in two parts." Toff's voice was now lighthearted, but I could see that he was nervous; his hand shook. "Everybody, I'm gay."

Jess and Caitlin didn't bat an eye. Carson looked puzzled. "Wait," he said. "What the hell, Toff? First Geordi and now you?"

Toff raised both hands. "Hold on, Carson. That was just part one. Now for part two." He reached over, took my hand, and I just about pulled my head into my neck like a turtle. "Geordi and I are in love with each other."

Carson's mouth fell open.

Jessica clicked her tongue loudly. "Yeah, yeah, congrats and warm fuzzies. But please, Toff. Like that's news. Anybody with half an eye who's known the two of you for the past couple of months could see you were hot for Geordi and he was hot for you."

Carson turned an incredulous gaze on Jess. "I've known them for a couple of years and I've got two *good* eyes and I didn't see it."

"Now wait a minute," I broke in. I was going to say Jess was wrong, at least about me being hot for Toff. But with Toff standing right beside me clasping my hand all lovey-dovey, it didn't take a fortune teller to know what such a pronouncement would do to the guy. I shut my mouth and kept it closed.

"Come on, Geordi. You and Toff have been punching and pushing each other around for almost a year. I know love taps when I see 'em," Jess went on. "What is it about boys that makes it so the only way they can show affection between themselves is by beating the crap out of each other? That's so Neanderthal."

"Yeah," Caitlin agreed. "The grown-up way to go when two people have a thing for each other is to just haul off and kiss." She got to her knees, leaned over, and planted a long, hungry smooch on Jess's lips.

And, like Carson, Toff and I stood there with our mouths hanging open.

After they finished their kiss, Caitlin lay down with her head in Jessica's lap. The big, messy red smudge left on Jess's mouth looked like an ugly bruise, but Jess obviously didn't care about that. She looked totally happy. Both girls beamed innocently at us. "Oh, by the way, Toff," said Jessica, "you're not the only one coming out today. Caitlin and I are dating."

Carson shook his head as if the house had just tilted ninety degrees. "What the fuck? Am I the only straight kid in this whole damn neighborhood?"

I WAS coasting along on my latest trip to the Land of Milk and Madness.

After the whole lesbian coming-out thing, I learned that Caitlin—whose chest alone knocked the *V* out of voluptuous and who wore more paint on her face than most clowns—was a practicing Catholic. Who would have guessed that? She had choir rehearsal at six and left Toff's after a final round of Uno. Jessica left too, walking hand in hand with Caitlin to the church. Jess hated organized religion; she declared it was all about bullying people, especially those who chose not to participate. By her own admission, she hadn't set foot in a church since her christening when she was barely a year old. Now there she was trotting off to Saint Mary's Cathedral with her new girlfriend.

Crazy.

But my world was about to get even crazier. Batshit crazier.

"So what do you guys want to do now?" Carson asked after the girls departed. "And if you say you're gonna hug up and stuff, I'm out."

"I should be getting home," I said, getting up from the floor where we were sitting. "It's almost dinnertime."

Carson's entire body seemed to perk up. "What're you having?"

"I don't know. Probably some soy-based dish. My mom doesn't cook a lot of meat."

"Can I have dinner with you?" Carson asked eagerly.

I looked at him as if his brain had oozed out his ear. "You want to eat tofu surprise?"

"Man, my mom is out of town, and my dad can't cook worth a damn. Yesterday, the man burned canned soup—*soup!*—and I had to eat it because he refused to fix anything else. So if I got a choice between what your mom's cooked and what my dad burned up today, I'll take the toe-whatever surprise."

"Well…." I shrugged. "My mom and dad tell me my friends are always welcome. I guess they'll let you in too. So if you don't mind yuppie food, follow me." Wait. Did I just invite Carson Meyer to come home with me? Yeah, I've definitely gone off the rails.

"Awesome! Thanks, Geordi. Let me call my dad and tell him to count me out for dinner." He pulled out his phone and scurried off into a corner to make his call.

I took Toff by the hand and led him into the foyer to make sure Carson didn't overhear us. "What's up with your dad, man?"

"Geordi, I don't want to talk about him."

I was too worried to let it go. "We have to talk about him, Toff. He's gone AWOL. Doesn't that make you even a little nervous?"

"I told you, he's done this before."

"Okay, but this is two days he's been gone now."

Toff's face shut down. It went completely blank, and I knew I wasn't going to get another word out of him about his father. "Come on home with me," I said. "We'll have dinner and you can spend the night again."

"I'll have dinner, but I'm sleeping here tonight."

"By yourself?"

"Come on. It's not like I'm two years old, Geordi."

"Agh!" I growled, snatching away from him. "You drive me freaking insane sometimes!"

Toff seemed confused. He always looked helpless when he was confused. "What're you mad at me for?"

I couldn't have explained it. I didn't know why resentment had been nagging at me all afternoon, like a low-grade fever. This wasn't just anger at myself for not kissing Jake; it was much more than that.

"It's not like I don't want to stay at your house," Toff explained. "I'd rather be with you even if my dad were here now. I only… don't be mad at me, Geordi."

With a deep breath, I pushed back the anger. "Look, I'm sorry. I just don't like the idea of you being here all night with your dad gone. Stay at my house. It'll be fun."

"I don't want to tell your parents that my dad isn't back yet. I don't want them to know."

"We don't have to tell them that's why you're spending the night. I'll make up something." I looped my arm around his neck the way I'd done hundreds of times before. "Come on. What do ya say?"

A slow smile spread across his face. "I say okay." Toff moved in and kissed me.

"Whoops!" Carson, who had just walked into the foyer, did a sharp about-face, his hands over his eyes. "No worries, fellas. I didn't see that."

"WELL, CARSON, it's so nice you've graced us with your company again," said Dad. He looked as delighted as a little kid with a new pony.

"I want to thank you and Mrs. Quintrell for having me, sir." Carson turned on his I'm-such-a-polite-and-lovable-boy smile, the one reserved for adults he wanted to suck up to. "And I really love these furry toad backs."

"That's *curry tofu bites*," Mom corrected pointedly. Her voice sounded peeved. She didn't like jokes about her cooking.

Not that Carson was joking. "Yeah, that. Yum!" He shoveled a big spoonful of braised and glazed tofu into his mouth and chewed, looking every bit as happy as my dad. And I decided then that I would never eat anything Carson's dad cooked. Ever.

"I'm curious, Carson," Dad said. "You don't come around the house as often as some of Geordi's other friends. Why is that?"

"I don't know, Mr. Quintrell." Carson turned to me, all innocent smiles. "Geordi, why don't you invite me over more often?"

Because you're a Class A asshole. "Hey, Mom, Dad, Toff's gonna spend the night again, if it's okay with you. There's this new graphic novel coming out tomorrow, and we want to get to the bookstore first thing in the morning so we can pick up our copies."

"Well, that's fine, Geordi," Dad replied. "I'll get the air mattress inflated."

Mom was studying Toff again. He didn't even notice it, eating mechanically as he looked around the dining room in this kind of vacant manner. "Toff, are you okay?"

He seemed to come to, focusing on Mom. "Huh? Oh sure, Mrs. Quintrell. I'm all right."

"Anybody want the rest of this toadstool?" Carson asked, eyeing the last bit of tofu in the serving dish.

Dad laughed. "Help yourself, kiddo." He laughed again as Carson eagerly dumped the remaining tofu on his plate.

Mom wasn't pleased with the steady stream of malapropisms regarding one of her signature dishes. "You boys clean up the kitchen."

Thanks a lot, Carson.

CARSON WAS on clearing-the-table duty. Toff was washing, and I was drying and putting away. There's an electric dishwasher in our kitchen, by the way, and it's in perfect working order. It never got used, however. My mom, carbon footprints, and all that.

Toff and I were alone in the kitchen. He was filling the sink with hot water while I stood by waiting for the work detail to begin. "Did you actually tell your folks I'm staying over so we can go to the bookstore tomorrow?" Toff asked.

"Yeah. Why?"

"That's dumb, man. What does me spending the night have to do with going to the bookstore in the morning? We can still get to the store first thing whether I sleep here or at home."

"It worked, didn't it?"

"*Estúpido.*" He said it with a smile.

"*Idiota.*" I smiled right back at him.

"*Tonto.*"

"*Muerte cerebral.*"

With that, we exhausted all the Spanish insults we'd picked up from Jess. So I shoved Toff in the shoulder. He shoved me back. We tussled in front of the sink. The tussling turned into an embrace. And the embrace turned into kissing.

Neither of us heard the door from the dining room swing open.

But I distinctly heard Dad's confused voice. "Geordi?"

Toff and I turned. Mom and Dad were standing in the open doorway holding stacks of dirty dishes and looking surprised as hell. They were helping clear the table with Carson, who stood in front of them holding his own stack of dishes. Carson was eyeing the floor in a way that said, *I don't want to get caught in the middle of this crap.*

"What is this?" Mom asked, looking from me to Toff.

"I thought...," Dad sputtered at me. "Didn't you say you were...?"

I was the *muerte cerebral* at the moment, unable to form a coherent thought in my head. Toff took on the duty of answering for the both of us. "Mr. and Mrs. Quintrell, I'm gay. And I'm also Geordi's boyfriend."

Mom and Dad looked as if they were going to take off and fly around the kitchen. "Oh my God. That's wonderful!" Dad cried.

Mom shoved her stack of dishes on one of the counters, rushed over, and threw her arms around Toff and me. "Boys, I'm so happy you came together. It's perfect because you've been friends for so long. When in the world did all this happen?"

"I've been in love with Geordi for a long time," Toff answered, "but we only made it official a couple of days ago."

Smiling, Mom put her hands on her hips and narrowed her eyes at me in a way that sniped, *You scamp!* "I knew there was something going on with you two. I didn't buy that line about going to the bookstore in the morning for one minute."

Dad put down his stack of dishes and grabbed Toff's hand. "Sandor Toffler, my boy, welcome to the family."

Toff was grinning like a maniac. "Wow. Thanks, Mr. Quintrell."

"Oh hell. Call me Pop." Dad pinched Toff's cheek. "Son."

I closed my eyes for a moment, wishing I'd just melt away. *Really, Dad?*

"Geordi, I agree with your mother," Dad said, patting me heavily on the back as if I'd just won a championship or something. "It's great that you and Toff have each other. We have to celebrate this momentous happening. We should throw a big par—"

"Dad! You and Mom. Out!" I took them each by an arm and practically dragged them toward the living room. "You go relax, watch TV, take a walk together or something. Kitchen cleanup is on me and my boys."

"Uh, Mr. and Mrs. Quintrell, I'm not Geordi's 'boy' boy, you know," Carson was quick to point out. "That would be Toff. I'm just Geordi's boy. Pal. Bud. No three-way stuff going on here. Because I'm straight. You know. Uh… that doesn't count against me, right?"

Yup. Asshole. Class A.

"Oh wait," Dad said, pulling away from me. "I have to get a picture of you, Geordi, with your new boyfriend."

"Dad, the kitchen—"

"It'll only take a second, and then you boys can get to work." He tugged out his phone and then started motioning for Toff and me to get together in a pose of some sort.

I rolled my eyes.

"Come on, Geordi." Toff walked up and got beside me. He took my hand and we stood there smiling. Only Toff's smile was genuine. Mine felt like a cardboard cutout.

Dad aimed his camera lens our way. Carson, being as much of a glory hog off the court as he is on the court, couldn't resist the opportunity to horn in. Just as Dad snapped the picture, Carson bumped me with his hip, knocking me sideways. I stumbled past Toff and barely managed to catch my balance before hitting the wall.

"Carson!" I would have followed that with some major cussing, but my parents were standing there.

"Don't blame me, dude," Carson said, grinning. "You know you've never been able to take a hit."

WE WERE watching TV in the living room, Mom, Dad, Toff and me. The kitchen was clean, Carson had gone home, and the sun was setting.

Jurassic World was playing on the screen. Mom and Dad made the concession in honor of my new relationship status. Rampaging dinosaurs, screaming people, chaos and destruction all around—that's my kind of movie. But I couldn't focus on the action. Toff and me. Mom and Dad knew all about that now. If I broke things off with Toff, I'd not only hurt him, I'd hurt my parents too. I felt as if I were sinking in the middle of the ocean with a half-ton weight strapped to my legs.

"I'm going to have some sherbet," Mom announced. "Anyone else?"

"Me," I said. *Maybe that'll take my mind off my crappy life for a minute.*

"Me too," said Toff.

"Make that four," said Dad.

"Come on, Geordi," Mom said. "Give me a hand."

In the kitchen Mom went for the freezer and I went to the cabinet for bowls.

"Honey, what's going on with Toff?"

The question sent a trill of anxiety through me. I had to tread carefully here. "What do you mean?"

"Something's off with him. I can't put my finger on it. He's always seemed a little sad to me. But now he's... lost. Or something." She brought the carton of sherbet to the counter where I'd set out the bowls. "Has he told you anything?"

In that I'd asked Toff repeatedly about his dad without getting any real answer, I could answer Mom truthfully. "No."

"Well, he won't talk to me. I'm sure he'd be more comfortable with you. See if you can get him to open up, honey. If something's wrong and there's anything I can do to help him, I certainly will."

I was as worried about Toff as Mom was, and I didn't bother trying to hide it. "Okay, Mom. I will."

"GOOD NIGHT, Mom, Dad."

"Yeah, good night."

"Good night boys. Sleep well."

Toff and I walked down the hall to my room. We both stopped short. "Hey, Dad, you didn't put the air mattress down on the floor."

"That's because Toff is sleeping in the guest room."

I looked up the hall at Mom and Dad, puzzled. "He always sleeps on the air mattress in my room when he stays over."

"Well, honey," said Mom, "you don't seriously think we'll let you boys sleep together in the same room now that you're boyfriends. Do you?"

"But Toff and I aren't having sex."

Mom smirked. "Exactly."

CHAPTER 9

THE NEXT day, Toff didn't seem to want to go home.

We ate Pop-Tarts for breakfast and lunch and in-between snacks. We played a couple of games of H-O-R-S-E in the driveway, binged on some episodes of *The Walking Dead*, and skinny-dipped in the pool.

I'm still amazed Toff and I got into that last one. I wasn't exactly for it at first.

"It'll be fun," he said.

"Me naked in public is no fun."

"This isn't public. It's your backyard. Nobody else is here."

"You're here."

Toff got this sober look on his face, almost like he'd done something wrong and wanted to make up for it. "Okay, I get it, Geordi. You're self-conscious, you think you're the opposite of hot. And I don't want you doing anything you're not ready for. But dude, you are totally wrong about your body. I think you look good, in *and* out of clothes. I notice the way you hold back sometimes when we're making out, and I get that too. I'm ready for sex but you're not, and I'm cool with that. You don't have to worry because I will never push you. When you're comfortable being naked with me, when you're ready, I'm all there."

Okay. Points for sincerity, for understanding my body shame, and for not pressing on the whole let's-get-nekkid-and-sex-it-up thing. Also, it didn't hurt that he'd said I was sexy. What with the way he'd grabbed me after our first date, and the way he was looking at me now, I actually started thinking that maybe I was, in some sense of the word, *hot*. "Thanks, man." I smiled at him. Then I stared. At his chest. At his legs. Toff was hot as hell in clothes. And if he was that exciting dressed....

Hmm.

Nah, it wouldn't be fair to ask him to get naked while I kept my clothes on. "So, you really want me to skinny-dip with you, huh?"

"Only if you want to, Geordi."

"We promised my parents we wouldn't have sex if they left us here alone today."

"Who said anything about sex? We'll just be swimming."

"Only swimming?"

He raised his right hand as if he were on the witness stand in some courtroom. "Swear to God."

In a giddy, excited rush, I started stripping down in my backyard. Toff was caught completely flat-footed. He just stood there at first with that I-can't-believe-my-eyes expression on his face. Then he started tearing off his clothes.

Oh. Uh. *Yes.*

I'd never seen Toff naked before, and I have to admit, it was a pleasant treat and a literal eye-opener. The sight of his strong, pale bare body made it very hard—in every sense of the word—to keep the promise I'd made to my parents before they left home this morning. It was a definite look-but-don't-touch situation. I had to jump in the water to take things down a notch. We swam, we chased each other around the deck in a duel of water bazookas, and I loosened up enough to where I was having a pretty good time. The whole episode made me feel closer to Toff than ever. There was something about intentionally sharing myself with him in a way I'd never done with anyone else. It was exquisite, being naked with him.

Then the theme from *Star Wars* intruded. I retrieved my cell phone from the pocket of my discarded jeans and saw the name "Bernard Caple" on the caller ID. What the hell? I'd called the Caples' house a few times to tell them I was bringing over misdelivered mail or that their garbage bin had blown over in their backyard, but they'd never called me before. I thumbed the Talk icon. "Hello."

It was Mrs. Caple on the line. "Just so you know," she said without preamble, "I can see you boys from my bedroom window." Then she laughed and disconnected.

Eek.

There was a privacy fence around the backyard, lined with thick hedges to boot. Who knew my elderly neighbor had x-ray vision? Oh wait. Dag. Maybe her bedroom is *up*stairs, and she can see *over* the fence.

"Geordi?" Toff looked at me closely. "Who was that?"

"Mrs. Caple."

"Who?"

"Mrs. Caple. You know her, the neighbor who lives behind me. I hide in her tree sometimes. She's like, in her seventies. She called to say she can see us."

"You mean… now? She can see us naked?"

"Yeah."

"Oh. Well, I guess we're giving her a thrill, huh?"

"Toff, she laughed when she told me."

"Laughed?"

"*Laughed.*"

"I think I'm ready to go inside now."

"I think I'm ready to crawl under my bed and die."

AROUND MIDAFTERNOON, in my room, Toff was surfing comic book sites on my iPad while I hunched over my phone, texting with Jake. So far, Toff hadn't said anything about going home, and he hadn't checked for messages from his dad. I didn't have the first clue on how to get him to open up.

ButchJake: Need to c u.

LaForge: Y?

ButchJake: Got stuff to talk about.

LaForge: Text.

ButchJake: No. Talk. Face 2 face. I'm outside your house.

I sat up like a dog at attention.

LaForge: NOW?

ButchJake: Yes now.

LaForge: Somebody drove u?

ButchJake: Took Mom's car, drove myself.

LaForge: WTF?

ButchJake: No license, no permit. Go 2 jail if caught.

LaForge: U r crazy!

ButchJake: Really need to c u. Can I come in and talk?

LaForge: Not a good time. Friend is here. What up?

ButchJake: Really confused 2day. Want so bad to do stuff with a guy.

My heart skipped.

LaForge: Maybe u should go ahead, try it.

ButchJake: Who with?

LaForge: ???

ButchJake: U got a gay friend 4 me?

I didn't know a single gay dude aside from Toff, and I wasn't about to share him. Not that he wanted to be shared.

LaForge: Sorry no.

ButchJake: OK. Maybe we can talk another time?

LaForge: Another time 4 sure.

ButchJake: Going now.

I listened. Outside, a car engine churned to life, the sound muffled by the walls of the house. The sound receded and faded out. When I tossed my phone aside, I noticed Toff watching me. "What's wrong?" he asked.

"Nothing."

"You look like you're angry or something. Kinda sad."

"No, I'm okay. Come on. Let's go to your house."

Toff sighed and looked away. "I don't want to."

"You have to go home eventually. Might as well be now."

"Why? Can't we just hang out some more, you and me?"

"Come on, man. Grab your backpack and let's go."

We walked the distance to Toff's house in silence. As I expected, his father's car wasn't in the driveway. Toff tossed his backpack on the porch and sat down on the steps. He leaned forward, forearms braced across his knees, staring at his feet.

I stood in front of him. "Where's your dad, Toff?"

"I don't know."

"Tell me what's wrong."

Being back at his house seemed to change him. The shell he'd put on at my place fell away. Fear surfaced in his eyes, so sudden and strong it made his face go pale. Panic was only a few heartbeats away. He put his hand over his mouth as if to smother a scream.

My own panicky feelings started up, a frantic flutter in my stomach. I sat down beside Toff and put my arm around his shoulders. "What is it, man? Please tell me. If you really want me for a boyfriend, you can't shut me out. Tell me what's going on with your dad."

Toff squeezed his eyes tight, his hand still over his mouth. After a moment, he pulled his hand away and opened his eyes. "He left me," he said in a quiet voice.

"What?"

"My dad left me. I checked his room yesterday. All his clothes and stuff are gone. He must've had them packed in the trunk that morning he said he was going off to fish. He kept emergency cash in a fake can in the kitchen cabinet. I checked it and the can is empty. He took all the money."

"Wait. I don't get it. You're saying he went off on some kinda trip? When's he coming back?"

"He's not coming back, Geordi."

A single tear spilled from Toff's left eye and ran down his cheek.

THE AIR was still and hot. The sun beat down full strength, unhindered by any clouds. Toff started shaking, and even when I wrapped both arms tight around him, I couldn't make it stop. I dug his key from his pocket, got him up, and took him inside.

His skin felt strange, cold and damp. "Here, lie down." I guided him to the sofa. He lay down on his back. Then he turned on his side and curled into a trembling ball. I went to his room, grabbed the comforter off his bed, and covered him up to his neck. Was he in shock? What do you do for a person who's in shock?

Several moments later he stopped shaking. He stared straight ahead, looking completely exhausted.

I knelt on the floor in front of the sofa and put my hand on his shoulder. "Toff, are you okay?" I asked softly. "You want me to get you something?"

He shook his head.

"Why do you think your dad's not coming back? People get stressed, especially adults. Sometimes they just need to get away for a while. You know, to readjust and all. You said yourself that your dad's taken off before, and he always came back."

Toff looked at me, his eyes hollow with anxiety. "All his stuff is gone, Geordi. All the stuff that matters, anyway. He's never done that before, taken everything with him. At that construction company where he works, three days off the job without calling in automatically gets you fired and replaced. It's been three days now, and Dad never called in. I checked that too."

"Do you have any idea where he's gone? Any friends he might shack up with?"

"No, no."

"What about relatives?"

"The only relatives I know of are on my mom's side. Dad cut off all contact with them after Mom died. Or maybe they cut off contact with us. I don't know."

"Well, you know any of their names, or how to get in touch with them?"

"No."

Shit. "Your dad doesn't have any friends? A fishing buddy? A girlfriend?"

"If he does, he never told me about them."

Well, I was fresh out of ideas. "Toff, we have to do something."

"I don't want to tell your parents—"

"My mom already suspects there's a problem, and she's not just gonna let this go. She wants to help you. You know how she is, how she can see through a lie."

"What if she wants to call the police?"

"Maybe we *should* call the police. Maybe your dad is somewhere hurt, and that's why he hasn't gotten in touch."

Toff looked like he wanted to cry again. "I don't know. I don't know what I want to do."

"You have to do something, Toff. The situation sure as hell isn't gonna get any better by itself."

He sniffed, falling silent for a moment while he apparently ran options through his head. "Maybe… maybe I can just stay here for a while. Not say anything to anybody. Give myself a chance to figure out what to do."

"How's that supposed to work? You said your dad took all the money. How will you buy food and pay the gas, electric, and water bills? If you can't pay the rent or mortgage or whatever, you'll get kicked out." I immediately regretted saying that because Toff sat up with a frightened groan, his lips trembling. "Okay. We don't have to do anything right now. You're right. We need to take some time and figure out what our first move should be."

"Don't tell your parents yet, please, Geordi. All right? If we have to, we can always tell them later."

"What about Jess? Is it okay if I tell her? She's pretty good at thinking up ideas in a pinch."

"Yeah, that's okay. You can tell her. But nobody else."

Great, Toff. That'll make it easier to deal. "Listen. I have to go check on something. Will you be okay here by yourself for a while?"

"I can come with you."

"No. You look wasted. Why don't you just chill? I won't be gone long."

"Where are you going?"

"To your dad's job. I'm gonna ask around to see if anyone there knows anything about where he's gone."

Toff stood up. "I'm definitely coming with you."

WE TOOK the bus that traveled the Poplar Avenue corridor. The main office of Magnum Home Builders was in a professional plaza a few blocks past East Parkway.

Toff looked pale and tired as we exited the bus and made our way across the parking lot. "Let me do the talking," he said with unusual firmness. I wasn't about to argue.

We pushed through double glass doors into the cool-air comfort of a sprawling, open-floor office. Five big desks surrounded by overstuffed chairs were spaced around the room. There was a sales associate seated behind each of those stations, and at two stations, the associates were actively engaged with customers seated across from them. At the front of the room, across from the main entrance, a smaller, sleeker desk held sway with a smiling guy receptionist in his early twenties who eyed us eagerly as we entered. "Hi there. What can I do for you fellas?"

Toff put on a smile, but even looking at him in profile, I could see the pain beneath it. "Hi, I'm Sandor Toffler, Gerald Toffler's son. This is my friend Geordi."

The receptionist stood up and leaned over the desk to shake hands with us both. I liked him already. "Nice to meet you, Sandor, Geordi. You boys look like you got cooked out there. Want some water?"

"That'd be great," I said quickly, afraid Toff would turn down the offer. My mouth and throat felt as if they were lined with sand. "Thanks."

The guy walked over to a fancy-looking upright cooler in the corner to our left, opened the door, and collected two frosty bottles of water. He walked back and handed them to us. "Here you go. Now what brings you in today?"

"My dad sent me down to pick up the stuff he left here," said Toff.

"Oh, right. I got it together earlier today. It's in a box here." He went behind the desk again, bent down, and came up with a small cardboard box in his hands. He placed it on the desk in front of us. There wasn't much inside: a Baltimore Orioles baseball cap, an insulated coffee mug, a pair of shades, a broken keyring, and a silver belt buckle.

Toff stared down at the items as if he couldn't figure out what they were.

"We've been a little worried around here about your dad," the receptionist said, his smile dimming. "He was quiet the last couple of days he was here, more quiet than usual. When he stopped showing up, his supervisor called and called him but never got an answer or a return call. Is your dad all right?"

"Yeah, he's fine," Toff answered. "He's on a fishing trip down in the Delta. After that, he says he's gonna drive around to some of his usual hangouts."

The receptionist stopped smiling altogether. "Usual hangouts?"

"Yeah, you know, like… Hot Springs. And the other places he always talks about."

"Well, I wouldn't know," said the receptionist. "Mr. Toffler never talked to me all that much, not like he did to some of his coworkers. I guess the age difference kind of kept us apart."

"What would a man like Gerry have in common with a wet-nosed kid like you, Tom?"

Toff and I turned at the sound of the lighthearted but gruff voice. A man decked out in scuffed work boots, dusty jeans, and a dingy T-shirt had just walked through the main entrance. He had a sweaty blue bandana tied around his head and a thick mustache that had just about turned pure gray. He was in his fifties, but he had a lean, work-hardened build. "I keep telling you, boy," the man said with a laugh, "you need to mind your place around here."

"This is my place to mind, Cole," the receptionist said, gesturing at his desk with both hands. "I was just talking to Gerry's kid here, Sandor, about the trip Gerry's off on."

The man named Cole looked at Toff and me as if we'd just popped out of thin air. He pointed at Toff. "You're Gerry's son?"

"Yes, sir," answered Toff. "I came by to pick up my dad's stuff."

"Pick up his stuff? Where the hell is he?"

"He went fishing."

"You mean to say Gerry walked away from his job to go fishing?" Cole's tone was so skeptical it made me want to grab Toff by the arm and leave.

"Sandor was telling me that Gerry's off to the Mississippi Delta to do his fishing," said the receptionist, cutting in.

Cole's face tightened in confusion. "When did he do that?" he asked Toff.

"He left... uh, yesterday."

"Well, he must've made a hell of a quick visit to the Delta," scoffed Cole. "I just got a call from one of our guys working the Platinum Estates subdivision out past Selmer. He swears he saw Gerry's car turn off Highway 64 on Route 28Z this morning."

Toff walked right up to Cole. "Is the guy sure it was my dad's car?"

"I asked him that," Cole replied. "He said it was a brown 2001 or so Toyota Camry with 'Toflr 1' on the license plate."

The man was only fuzzy on the year. Mr. Toffler drove a 2005 Camry; the rest of the description was spot-on.

"What the hell's your daddy doing out there, sonny boy?" Cole asked suspiciously. "There's not much out that way except bears, deer, and open country."

"Hunting," I said loudly without thinking. "He's going hunting out there." I grabbed the box with Mr. Toffler's things off the desk and turned back to the receptionist. "Well, thanks a lot for this, and for the water. We have to be going. Have a wonderful day. Bye."

I spun around like a model on a runway and hurried through the double glass doors with Toff on my heels. I swear I could feel that man Cole's eyes burning into the back of my head like a laser.

CHAPTER 10

"ARE YOU freaking kidding me?" Nobody does shock and disbelief like Jessica. Her eyebrows arched so high they practically merged with her hairline. And she's got a big-ass forehead.

We were sitting in the tire swings that hung from the big oak tree in her backyard. Mr. Sanchez had put up the swings for Jess and her brother nearly a decade ago. The spot was far enough away from her house to ensure nobody inside would overhear us.

"I kid you not. The man just took off and left Toff without even telling him he was leaving. He's gone for good, and he didn't even take time for a see-ya-later with his son." I was angry again, so angry I was grinding my teeth. "Who does that, Jess? What kinda man does that to his own kid?"

"There has to be something more to this, Geordi. That can't be the whole picture."

"Whether it's the whole picture or not, Toff is screwed."

"Where is he now?"

"At his house, sleeping. Emotionally, he's wiped out. I'm going back for him later."

"He doesn't have any idea where his dad went?"

"We went to Mr. Toffler's job a while ago. Some guy who works for the company saw his car turn off Highway 64 on Route 28Z this morning past some town called Selmer. We need to get out there and see if we can find him."

Jess pulled out her phone and tapped away at the screen. A few seconds later, her eyebrows went up again. "The intersection of Highway 64 and Route 28Z is more than two hundred miles from here."

"Dag. Are you serious?"

"There's no bus that goes out there. Somebody will have to drive us." She looked toward her house. "I can ask my mom, or maybe even my knothead brother—"

"You can't tell your mom or Javier."

"Why the hell not?"

"That's the way Toff wants it. He says I can tell you, but nobody else for now. He doesn't want the police involved yet, and he's afraid if your mom or my parents find out, the first thing they'll do is call the cops."

"I guess I can understand why he feels that way. The police will probably bring in Child Welfare, and they'll probably try to stick him in a group home or something. But if we don't tell our parents and get one of them to drive us, how do we check out Route 28Z? We sure as heck can't walk all the way out there. And if we find Mr. Toffler, how do we get him to bring himself back home without another adult to talk some sense into him? He's not gonna listen to a bunch of kids."

"Toff can do it. Toff can convince him."

Jess spat something harsh in Spanish, probably a cuss word or two. "That man never cared about anything Toff had to say before. What makes you think he'll give a crap now?"

"That's how Toff wants to play this, Jess. No one else can know. I promised him that. We'll just have to figure some way to get out to Route 28Z on our own."

"Well, I didn't promise him a thing. I'll tell our parents if that's what it takes to get Toff's dad to go home."

"Speaking of our parents, how do we time this whole going-after-Toff's-dad thing if we don't tell them what we're doing? It'll take like, three hours just to get out to that intersection, and another three hours to get back to Memphis. And that doesn't include the time we'll spend looking around. It'll be dark in a few hours. If we go after Mr. Toffler today, it'll be midnight or later when we get home. My parents will ground me for life. But if we go in the morning, we'll have all day to look for him and we can get home before dark."

"It'd be best to go after Mr. Toffler today. He was seen at that intersection this morning, and I'm pretty sure he's moved on from there. So the longer we wait, the more of a head start he gets. It's no big deal to me. I can tell my mom I'm spending the night with a friend."

"Some of us have a problem lying to our parents, Jess."

"Who says I'd be lying? After we get back to town, I'll spend the night at Toff's. You could do the same."

I was about to argue with her on that point but her ringtone—Beyoncé's "Crazy in Love"—cut me off. She put her phone to her ear to answer the call. "Hello." She listened briefly and broke into a smile. "Hi, Papá."

She switched to Spanish, and I promptly tuned her out, digging my own phone from my pocket. For a moment, I considered calling Jake. I felt bad for the guy. Coming out may not have been the best experience of my life, but I was never confused about my sexuality. It was hard for me to imagine what Jake was going through, overcome by desires he didn't understand with no way to explore them. There wasn't much point in calling him now for what would most likely be only a short hi-and-bye kind of conversation. The crap situation with Toff's dad was sucking up all my oxygen. What kind of friend was I to Jake when I couldn't even give him a sympathetic ear?

I checked out Uber's website for an estimate on a trip from Toff's house to our desired destination and back. That estimate was eye-popping to a person of my limited funds, and riding Uber required a credit card to boot. I was fresh out of credit cards.

Jessica's conversation with her dad took a sudden loud turn. I looked at her and saw that she'd become agitated, her eyes fiery and her lips curling with anger. What the hell was her father saying to her? She rattled off a long, rapid stream of heated Spanish that ended with "Goodbye, Papá! Maybe I *won't* see you then!" And with that she curtly disconnected the call.

For a second there, I thought she was going to throw her phone down. She shoved it into her pocket and went "Agh!"

"Jess, what's wrong?"

"That man!" she snapped before spiraling off into another explosion of Spanish.

"English, Jess. English."

She shut her mouth, taking a moment to force her face into a portrait of sweetness that was as fake as it was frightening. "My wonderful dad, the wonderful Señor Santiago Vicente Sanchez, called to say that he's coming to town next month for my quinceañera."

"Wow. That's… great?"

"My wonderful brother, the wonderful Javier Jesús Sanchez, sent my wonderful dad a photo of me and my truly wonderful new girlfriend, who my wonderful dad knew nothing about because I hadn't told him yet. So, after telling me he'll be here for my quinceañera, my wonderful papá went on to say he was surprised at how confused I was. He told me I am becoming a young woman, not a young man, and that if I know what's good for me, I'll have a wonderful *boy*friend by my side at the quinceañera."

Jess glared at me. I didn't open my mouth, afraid of saying the wrong thing and having all the anger pent-up behind her glassy-eyed stare blast me into orbit.

"Sorry." Jessica raised both hands, closed her eyes, and took a deep breath. She blew it out in a long sigh. After that she actually seemed to be calm. "No need for me to be upset because nobody controls my life but me. This is *my* quinceañera, celebrating me, *all* of me. Anybody who can't celebrate that can just stay away, including Señor Santiago. Okay. Now, Geordi, what were we talking about?"

Warning bells were still going off in my head, but I opened my big yap anyway. "There's something else… about Toff."

"And what's that?"

"Uhm… here's the thing. I'm not in love with him, not like he is with me."

"You're not?"

"No."

One corner of her mouth crooked up in a knowing smirk. What the hell was that about? "Really, Geordi? Do you really not know what's in here and here?" She touched her finger to my temple, then to my heart. "I can see it plain as day."

I scratched my scalp hard. "You can see what plain as day?"

Jessica let her head fall forward in this sort of hopeless way. "*God,* boys are so dense. How do people like you even breathe on your own?"

None of what she said made sense to me, and I didn't waste time trying to figure it out. "I don't know what to do, Jess. Toff told my parents that he's my boyfriend, and now they're all happy that I'm in my first relationship, which isn't really a relationship. On the one hand, I feel stuck in a place I don't want to be, and I want to get out of it. On the other hand, I don't want to hurt Toff, especially now with all the stuff he's going through, and I don't want to disappoint my parents either. I'm going crazy here. I don't know how to get myself out of this. I mean, don't I deserve to be happy with my life at least every now and then?"

The portrait of sweetness came back.

Uh-oh.

"You know, Geordi, sometimes you have this wonderful habit of turning everything around to you-you-you when it should be about something-something-something else. And I know your parents sometimes make everything about you-you-you, and maybe that's where this wonderful habit of yours comes from, and most times I just kinda overlook it and let you be a wonderful little self-centered yo-yo. But you know what, I'm not in the mood to overlook it today. Right now I think the focus should be on Toff-Toff-Toff, so why don't you get the freak over your wonderful self, step down off your royal throne, and *focus on Toff*! How about that?"

Yup. Should've listened to those warning bells.

I LEFT Jessica's house in a daze. I'd never been spanked, but I imagined this was what a little kid felt like in the aftermath: chastened and embarrassed. There was so much whirling around in my head—Toff's abandonment, our lopsided love affair, Jake's sexual identity issues—and it left me as confused as ever. Getting Jess pissed off at me didn't exactly help things either. Also still freaking me out was the timing of this trip. I didn't have a curfew or anything, but my parents expected me to be in the general vicinity of the neighborhood come nightfall. And by 10:00 p.m., I should be in the house or at least in my own yard. Jess was right; it would be best to go after Mr. Toffler this afternoon. But I couldn't just disappear for hours and leave my parents to worry themselves to death. Maybe if I went home, took a shower, and chilled for a minute, I could regroup and figure out what the hell I was supposed to do.

The sun was one harsh glare, and there wasn't even a hint of a breeze. I decided to take a shortcut across the campus of the elementary school where Mom taught. With my head down and my hands in my pockets, I tried to make myself as small as possible. I didn't want to be noticed. It would be nice if I could just fade into the background for a while.

"Faggot!"

The shout came from somewhere behind me. As the only friendly neighborhood homosexual in the immediate area, I instantly stopped and turned. Carson was marching across the campus toward me. My first reaction was frowning disbelief. Did Carson Meyer just drop the F-bomb on me? For a moment I was highly offended.

But only for a moment. Because then I saw how horribly pissed Carson was, his face twisted into the kind of primal hatred that had burned villages to the ground and sent whole populations running for the hills. And then I realized all that rage and hatred was directed exclusively at the only friendly neighborhood homosexual in the immediate area. And *then* Carson charged like the frontline of the New York Giants defense going after a Dallas QB.

I have to confess that, at fifteen, I was still a little afraid of Carson. He was bigger, stronger, and meaner than I was. With bigger, stronger, and meaner rushing me on a rocket of rage, I thought it was time to run for the hills myself.

I took off like the proverbial shot. My one advantage over Carson on the basketball court was that I was faster and more agile. I poured on speed, knowing my continued good health depended on it. As I ran my terror diminished slightly with the certainty that I was leaving Carson far behind in my dust trail.

A risky glance over my shoulder a few moments later slapped away my overconfidence in a single horrific instant. Carson was practically on my heels and steadily gaining. Something in his rage was fueling his muscles in a way mere sports cockiness never could. He reached out with his right arm, straining, and I saw with an awful sense of doom that he had me.

He caught me around the waist. With a single sharp motion of his arm, he flung me violently to my left. I slammed against a section of the chain-link fence surrounding the school's playground. As I bounced off, I was already thinking I would duck around Carson and take off again. But before I could get my balance, Carson grabbed the neck of my T-shirt and, with his fist at my throat, shoved me back against the fence.

"Stupid fag! Why'd you do it?" He shouted the question in my face and followed it immediately with his other fist. The blow landed on my nose and mouth, smashing the back of my head against the fence. A dry thickness seemed to explode in my sinuses, as if a dust bomb had gone off in there, but I felt no immediate pain.

I opened my eyes just in time to see Carson draw back for another punch. *Block it.* My hands started coming up almost simultaneously with that thought. The punches landed on my jaw before I could get my hands in place, however, a rapid-fire one-two-three. I definitely felt those blows, the pain shooting down into my neck.

"What'd I do?" I managed to shout, terrified and confused as hell, trembling hands up now to protect my face.

"Don't fucking stand there and pretend like you don't know!" He grabbed the front of my shirt with both fists and threw me down. I hit the ground on my shoulder and hip, landing so hard my body actually rolled over three times. That put a little distance between me and Carson, and I saw my opportunity to jet again. I scuttled like an oversized crab, got to my feet, and ran.

Carson was on my ass like a hungry bird on a bug. He was too close, moving too fast, and I knew I couldn't get away from him. Still, I kept running, shouting over my shoulder, "Wait! Wait!" *Take a minute to at least tell me what the problem is before you kill me!*

He landed a powerful punch right between my shoulder blades, knocking me off stride. I went down hard on the asphalt in front of the west entrance of the school.

When I was in third grade, I got into a shoving match with a boy named Phil Gottfried outside this entrance on a quiet autumn morning. Our teacher, Mrs. Glass, stepped in before things could escalate. It was the closest I'd come to being in an actual fight.

Until now, that is.

Carson loomed over me, his face one big snarl, his fists raised, his intent terrifyingly clear. I curled up, closed my eyes, and covered my head with my arms. He kicked me in the side and then rained down blows, his fists pounding in my chest, stomach, and face as I lurched and rolled, trying to minimize the damage. Calling this a fight was a gross exaggeration. A slaughter was more like it.

Carson dropped down, planting his knee in my back, pinning me to the ground. "How could you do that to me?" he shouted. "Huh? How could you do it? My dad saw the fucking pictures on Facebook. Now he thinks I'm goddamned gay!" He broke down, heaving in angry sobs.

I got the hell beat out of me, and the hell-beater was the one in tears.

What's wrong with this picture?

"I'm sorry, man. I'm sorry," I mumbled, even though I still wasn't sure what I was apologizing for.

He grabbed the back of my shirt, pulled me up, and flung me away from him. I stumbled, struggling for balance, trying not to fall again. "Don't be sorry!" he snapped. "Just get the fuck away from me!"

I didn't hesitate.

I ran.

ONCE I was in the house, I went straight to the bathroom and looked in the mirror.

It was a god-awful sight.

My upper lip was swollen and split. Blood from my nose and lip was streaked down my chin and the front of my shirt. Bruises were darkening around my left eye and along my jaw. My side, chest, and back ached from blows that had landed there. The knuckles on my right hand were scratched up. Hmm. How did that happen? It certainly wasn't from punching Carson.

My nose was still bleeding. I grabbed a towel, placed it over my nose, pinched my nostrils shut, and became a mouth-breather for about ten minutes. I wanted comfort, but there was none to be had. Mom was at the library. She volunteered three afternoons a week reading stories to preschoolers. Of course, Dad was at work. Not that I wanted him.

Once the bleeding stopped, I got out of my scuffed and blood-spattered clothes, stuffed them in the hamper, and took a shower. Walking naked and damp into my room, I spotted a bow-covered package on my bed. Curious, I ripped open the package and found a box of condoms, along with a note: "Before anything happens, let's talk about you and Toff and sex. Love, Mom." If my head weren't already hurting from Carson's pounding fists, I think that would have given me a migraine.

After stashing Mom's little present in my desk drawer, I dressed in clean clothes, sat down on my bed, and grabbed my iPad. I hadn't been on my Facebook page in a couple of days, and the only pictures Carson and I had ever been featured in together were some of the ones Dad took yesterday. I pulled up Dad's Facebook page.

And there it was. Under a banner that read "Meet Geordi's Boyfriend!" was the first picture Dad had taken of Toff and me, the one where Carson jumped in and bumped me halfway to Kentucky. The result was a shot where it looked like Carson and I were joined hip to hip in some weird-ass dance with Toff shuffled off to the background. I could see where Mr. Meyer—and anybody else unfamiliar with the situation— would get the impression that Carson was the boyfriend mentioned above. Dad had told me he contacted Mr. Meyer through Facebook to invite Carson to my coming-out party. Apparently Mr. Meyer followed

up with Dad on Facebook, and the rest was the sorry history that had left
me bleeding all over the school playground.

While I sat there, staring at the iPad's screen, I think my vision
literally went red.

"GEORDI? YOU home?"

There were the usual sounds of Dad's arrival from work: the
clink of hanging his keys on the peg by the back door; the thump of his
briefcase landing on the kitchen table; the clatter of ice dispensing from
the fridge's icemaker into a glass. Every noise added to my growing
irritation. I shoved my phone in my pocket and my feet into a pair of
sneakers, and I marched to the kitchen.

Dad was standing by the fridge, drinking down a glass of ice water
while he stared at the day's mail spread out on the counter. He looked up
when I walked in, and his eyes widened with shock. Choking on that last
sip of water, he put the glass aside and came toward me. "Geordi! What
happened to you?"

I could barely breathe, I was so angry. "What happened to me,
Dad? What happened? *You're* what happened."

"What're you talking about, son?" He reached out to take me by
the shoulders. "You look as if you got into a fight."

I jerked back from him. "A fight? No, I didn't get into any fight.
You took a bunch of stupid pictures of me and Toff and Carson, and you
stuck 'em up on freaking Facebook for the whole world to see, and I just
got the *shit* kicked out of me because of you."

"Geordi… what—?"

"You do this all the time, jump all over my life and make it freaking
hell. Why'd you have to put those stupid pictures on Facebook? Huh? Why
do stuff like that? Why do you have to make such a big deal out of every
single little thing? Why can't you just leave me alone sometime?"

Dad looked at me helplessly. "Son, I don't have a clue what you're
talking about. Sit down here and talk to me, let me try to make heads or
tails of this." He grabbed a chair and pulled it out for me.

"I don't want to talk to you! That's the problem. You stay in my
face so much it seems that I can't even breathe sometimes. I can't do
anything, period, with you around. I couldn't decide who I wanted to
come out to or when I wanted to come out to them because you decided

to do all that *your* way, not mine. What I wanted didn't even factor into the equation. You mess up everything for me. Everything!"

"Geordi, I don't know what's going on here, but you have to give me a chance to—"

"Just stay out of my life! You hear? I *hate* you!"

There was a frozen moment that seemed to narrow the space between us, giving every detail of my dad's slender face a stark and chilling clarity. Over the course of my life, I'd seen my dad in many moods. I'd seen him happy, pensive, upset, excited, sad, disappointed, and surprised. But I'd never seen him look so completely hurt as he did when those last three words flew from my mouth.

I couldn't stand it. I couldn't stand him. I couldn't stand the pain in his face, the woeful quiver of his mouth, the round, pathetic wounds that were his eyes. I dashed past my dad and out the back door.

He came after me. "Geordi, stop. Come back!"

For a man closing in on forty, Dad was still pretty quick on his feet. But he was nowhere near as quick as me.

I poured on the speed and left him far behind in my dust trail.

CHAPTER 11

I STOPPED at the edge of Jessica's front yard and dialed her number on my phone, reluctant to knock and risk having Mrs. Sanchez or Javier see me.

"What's up, Geordi?"

"I'm out front at your place."

"Okay. I'll be out in a second."

I sat down on the grass to wait. My jaw and nose and chest and side ached. Anger made me grind my teeth, clouding my mind and hurting my jaw even more. It beat in my chest, pulsed through my veins, tingled along my nerves. Jess and I had agreed I'd return to her house after I came up with a way to get her, Toff, and me to the intersection of Highway 64 and Route 28Z. I didn't have any such plan, and I was too agitated to come up with one.

There was motion behind me. Jessica ran over as lightly and quietly as a cat. "Hey."

I didn't look up at her. She bent down beside me. "Sheez. What happened to you?"

"I don't want to talk about it."

"Your face—"

"You said focus on Toff. So let's focus on Toff." I got up and marched off. Jess quickly caught up and fell in step beside me. We weren't headed in Toff's direction, but Jess didn't say anything. I had no particular destination in mind; I just needed to move. Jessica projected her usual calm and confident demeanor. I envied her for that.

My phone chimed. I pulled it out and saw that I had a text message from Jake.

ButchJake: What up?

I thumbed in a response as I walked.

LaForge: On my way 2 c friend. Where r u?

ButchJake: At mall. In trouble. Mom found out I took her car.

LaForge: Nice knowing u.

ButchJake: LOL

LaForge: Got things 2 do. Have 2 go now.
ButchJake: OK. Crying here. Lots of tears and snot.

Now I wanted to be in two places at once. That got me even angrier, and I pounded my fist against my thigh. Jess gave me a strange look.

LaForge: Sorry. I promise we will talk soon.
ButchJake: What do u have 2 do? Maybe I can help.
LaForge: U can't. Have 2 get friend 2 Hwy 64 & Rte 28Z asap.
ButchJake: I can do that. Still have Mom car.
LaForge: NO! U already n trouble.
ButchJake: So what's wrong with a little more?

DURING THE course of my text conversation with Jake, I decided I was through worrying about how my dad might feel. But I was sorry for how what I was about to do would worry Mom. I tucked my phone in my pocket, turned to Jess, and said. "Let's get Toff. We're going after his dad *now*."

WHEN JESS and I reached Toff's house, most of the neighbors' cars were in their driveways, and the scent of frying fish was wafting from next door. A bunch of little kids were having themselves a screaming, laughing good time running back and forth through a lawn sprinkler. The sun, still shining brightly, was starting to slide low in the west. The waning day left a sense of melancholy settling over my head. The anger that had driven me from home had mostly receded now, pushed aside by a growing swell of guilt. I wished I could take back what I'd said to Dad. This was why I tried to avoid saying how I really felt sometimes.

God, I am a rotten son. Bad to the core. But I wasn't about to back out of this now.

Jessica rang the bell. Toff opened the door moments later. He looked tired, his eyes half-closed, and he had a bad case of bed head, his hair smashed flat against his scalp on the left side. "Hi, Jess." Then he spotted me, and his mouth dropped open in alarm. "Geordi! What—?"

"Please, Toff, don't ask about the face," I said. "I'm okay, but I don't want to talk about it. Can we come in or what?"

"S-sure." He kept staring at me, the shock and concern in his eyes a good indication that my bruised face and split lip weren't looking any better.

I clasped my hands together at my chin in a begging gesture. "Can we *please* come in?"

"Sorry, sorry." He waved for us to follow, turned, and walked off, heading for the kitchen. I held the door for Jess and closed it once we were inside. We tromped off to the kitchen after Toff.

He opened the fridge and bent down to search the contents. "You guys want anything, a Coke or something?"

"No, I'm good," said Jess.

"Me too," I added.

Toff grabbed a can of Coke for himself and closed the fridge. Then he casually opened the freezer, grabbed a bag of frozen corn—as if that weren't his whole purpose in going to the fridge—walked over and gently placed the bag against the bruised half of my face.

"Thanks," I muttered as I raised my hand to hold the bag in place. Toff pulled me close and hugged me. That was exactly what I needed, and it warmed my heart even as half my head froze.

When he let me go, I said, "I told Jess everything that's going on with your dad."

"Okay." He gave her a wary look as he popped the tab on his soda. "What do you think?"

"Personally, Toff," Jess said, "I think we should bring in my mom or Geordi's parents. We need one of them to talk some sense into your dad."

"I just want to find him, Jess," Toff said. "Can we concentrate on that first?"

She shrugged. "Your call." She turned to me. "So, how're we easing on down Highway 64?"

Anxiety made my stomach growl. I checked the time on my cell phone. "Our ride should be here in about fifteen minutes."

WE STOOD on the porch and watched the dark gray Audi sedan as it rolled to a stop in Toff's driveway. I'd seen Mrs. Butcher's car a time or two before, and it was still as intimidating as it was when I first saw it. In movies this was the kind of vehicle funeral directors, FBI agents, and IRS auditors arrived in bearing briefcases stuffed with good news.

Seeing Jake's friendly, handsome face behind the wheel didn't ease my apprehension any. I was on the verge of introducing him to Toff. I was looking forward to that about as much as having a batch of spider eggs hatch in my ear.

Jessica walked out to the car first, followed by Toff, with me bringing up the rear. Jake powered down the driver's window and flashed a smile. Jess's eyes lit up with recognition. "I remember you," she said. "You were at Geordi's coming-out party."

Might as well get the fun part over with. I moved next to the driver's door. Jake looked up at me, and the smile dropped from his face like a rock. "Damn. Geordi, your face... what—"

"Don't ask, man. Just don't." I shook my head wearily and then took a deep breath to steel myself. "Toff, Jess, this is my bud Jacob Butcher."

"Hi," Jake said, waving his hand and smiling again. "Everybody calls me Jake."

"Jake, this is my best friend, Jessica Sanchez."

Jess stuck out her hand. "How ya doin', Jake?"

"I do just fine now that I've met you, Jess." He shook her hand warmly, and I'd almost swear she blushed at the charming bastard. Jess never blushed.

"And Jake, this is Sandor Toffler." I reached over and took Toff's hand. "He's my boyfriend."

Jake's smile froze for an instant, the only hint that some less than positive emotion had just floated beneath his pleasure. "Sandor. So you're the lucky dude," he said, shaking hands.

"Everybody calls me Toff."

"Good deal, Toff. It will be my pleasure to drive you guys this evening." Jake winked at the three of us.

PAST THE town of Oakland, Highway 64 cut through open, yellow-green plains against a backdrop of gently rolling hills and dense forest. There hadn't been any rain in nearly four weeks, and the grass in those plains was so dry a single spark would set off an inferno. Dots of civilization popped up occasionally—houses of various sizes tucked on carefully tended lots, a small, white clapboard country church, a sprawling redbrick school building. Traffic was very light. The sun had just dipped below the horizon behind us. The windows were down and the sunroof was open, allowing pleasantly warm breezes to blow through the sedan's cabin.

Under other circumstances, I would have been enjoying the ride.

"You're a good driver," Jessica said. She was sitting in the front passenger seat.

"Thanks," Jake replied. "My dad started teaching me when I was thirteen. My mom had a fit when she found out, but it didn't stop the lessons."

"Maybe my brother should've started at thirteen. He drives like a maniac. My mom didn't start teaching him until he was sixteen. He got his license six months later, and right off the bat he forgot everything he learned about speed limits and traffic signs."

"Well, that won't be happening with me, not on this trip. I don't want to get the attention of any cops."

Jessica froze for a beat, looking at Jake. "Something tells me I don't want to ask this question, but I'm asking anyway. Do you have a driver's license?"

"Nope. I'm fifteen. I don't even have a learner's permit. I don't have auto insurance either. And I'm not only driving-while-black, I took this car without my mom's permission, so technically, it's stolen. If the cops stop us, I'm going straight to jail."

Sitting in the back seat with Toff, I sighed. "Dude. Did you have to tell her all that?"

Jake flashed a quick grin over his shoulder at me. "Hey, I may be a lawbreaker, but I'm an *honest* lawbreaker."

Jess giggled. "You're funny, Jake. You just scared the hell out of me, but you're funny." She casually poked her thumb over her shoulder in my direction. "How'd you wind up making friends with Jerko Quintrell back there?"

"Our dads work together at the Pink Palace. They started dragging us to functions at the museum when we were about eight years old. The events were pretty dry for anyone under thirty. Geordi and I sorta kept each other from dying of boredom." He glanced quickly at Jess. "And how did you wind up becoming friends with Geordi?"

"Somebody put a curse on me."

"Fun-neee," I snapped. Toff and I were sitting close together, with Toff's hand resting on my thigh.

"What about you, Toff?" Jake looked back at us through the rearview mirror. "How long have you and Geordi been boyfriends?"

"Since the day after the coming-out party," said Toff.

Jake cocked an eyebrow. "You guys fell for each other pretty quick, huh?"

"No, actually I've had feelings for Geordi for a long time. I didn't know he was gay until the party, so I never said anything to him before. It turned out he loved me as much as I loved him, and that was that."

"Yeah, that's beautiful. I can understand why you didn't tell him before. The same thing happened to me. I had a crush on a guy in my neighborhood, but he's straight, so that was major frustration. When I found out Geordi's gay, I tried to talk him into making up for my disappointment with a big fat kiss."

Toff's fingers tightened on my thigh so hard I thought my kneecap would pop off like a champagne cork. Fighting back a squeal, I pried his hand loose.

Jake kept going, not unlike a natural disaster. "We didn't know each other all that well, and I figured a kiss would be a good way for us to start getting closer. Plus he's a lot hotter now than he was when we were eight, which would make kissing a whole lot more fun, so I thought, 'Why not?' You know what I mean?"

I cocked my head to one side, scowling at the back of Jake's noggin in utter disbelief. "Dude!"

"What?" Jake's gaze shifted in the rearview mirror to Toff, whose current expression would make a pretty good I'm-jealous-as-hell emoji. "Oh listen, Toff. You'll be proud of the guy. Geordi turned me down right off, said he was seeing someone and didn't want to hurt him. He didn't let me get anywhere near kissing those nice boy-lips of his."

The words were meant to reassure Toff, and they probably would have done their job if Jake hadn't winked over his shoulder at me. The wink was intended as an innocent gesture, conveying an unmistakable I-got-your-back message. I don't think Jake had a clue how conspiratorial that seemed.

But Toff sure did. His body stiffened beside me as he clamped his hand on my leg and dug his fingers in deep again. I thought he was going to leave his prints on my thigh bone. My eyes crossed and I went "Yeep!"

Jess leaned toward Jake in a move that foreshadowed the start of a new conspiracy. In a half whisper she said, "Come on, Jakey. You got a taste of those Geordi lips, didn't you? Sly guy like you can get anything off anybody, I'll bet. I can tell you kissed Geordi."

"In another lifetime, maybe, but not this one," Jake replied, his face all honest and a little sad. "If I had locked lips with him, maybe this feeling of wanting to kiss a guy would be gone. It's all I can think about lately."

Toff eased his grip on my leg, and I felt his body relax next to me. Jess looked back at me and winked. I mouthed, "Thank you."

"You never kissed a guy before, Jake?" Toff asked in a voice running over with sympathy.

"No. If you'd asked me eight months ago, I would've said I was plain old straight. Hell, if you'd asked me six weeks ago, I'd have said I was straight but curious about being with a guy. But now I'm like, all about wanting to be with a dude. I wonder if that means I'm turning gay."

"Are you still attracted to girls?" Jess asked.

"Yeah, sure. I think you're cute, Jess, by the way. I could definitely go for you."

"If you're still into girls, 'gay' isn't a word I'd apply to you." She looked over her shoulder. "Toff, Geordi, either of you guys ever been attracted to girls?"

"Nope," I said.

"Never," said Toff.

Jess looked at Jake. "See? *That's* gay."

Jake chewed at his lip for a moment. "So I guess that makes me… confused?"

"Why are you so set on labeling yourself? I've got a girlfriend now, but six months ago, I was into a guy named Taylor."

"Whatever happened to that guy, Jess?" asked Toff.

"I dumped him," Jess answered, looking annoyed at the interruption.

"Why?" Toff asked just as Jess was about to say something to Jake.

"He made a joke about 'fags.'" She disgustedly painted air quotes with her fingers. "I told him I didn't like jokes like that because my best friend is gay. He asked how I can be friends with a fag. I told him I'd rather be friends with a fag than a deadhead, and I dumped him."

"Wait a minute, Jess," I said, the implication of what she'd just said finally sinking into my head. "You told Taylor I'm gay before I—"

Jessica shot an impatient look over her shoulder. "Would you just chill, Geordi? I didn't mention you by name to Taylor. Sheez." She switched her attention to Jake once more. "The point I'm trying to make here is that I'm just like you, Jake. I'm attracted to boys and girls."

"You're bi," said Toff.

"No, I'm *me*. And I'm still figuring myself out. Until I do figure myself out, how would I even know who I am? I'm not ready to pick a label yet. If I did, I think I'd just be limiting myself."

Toff looked confused. "I don't get it. It's like you think bi is something to be ashamed of."

"That's not what I'm saying at all. I'm not ashamed of what I feel. I'm just trying to make sure I understand myself. And I don't want anybody telling me who I am, not even you, Toff."

"Okay, you're right, Jess. Sorry."

Jake was chewing on his lip, the sign of a guy thinking hard. I found myself feeling sorry for him again. "It's gonna be okay, man," I said, giving him a pat on the shoulder. "You'll figure yourself out."

"Yeah," he mumbled.

"So how does that work, Jake?" Toff asked. "Are you half attracted to girls and half attracted to guys?"

Jess groaned and shook her head, muttering, "Oh my God," under her breath.

Jake seemed to consider the question, taking a few moments before he answered. "I've been attracted to more girls than I have guys. For a while, I was just crushing on this straight dude in my neighborhood. Once I realized what a nowhere situation that was, I got attracted to Geordi. And then I started, like, daydreaming about getting busy with a guy, any guy."

"That doesn't sound 'confused' to me, man," Toff pointed out. "Sounds more like you know exactly what you want. I'm no expert, and I'm definitely not trying to stick you with a label you're not ready for. But seems to me you're probably bi."

"Well, here's one thing I definitely know about me," Jake said. He flipped on his turn signal and guided the car toward a gas station looming ahead. "I gotta pee, and I'm thirsty. Pit stop, people!"

"How's the gas gauge looking?" asked Jess.

"We're down to a fourth of a tank," Jake replied.

Jess threw a look over her shoulder at Toff and me. "Come on, guys. We should at least pay for a fill-up."

Toff and I agreed. While Jake pulled up to the pumps, Jess, Toff, and I dug through our pockets.

We came up with a grand total of $6.47, a paperclip, and a fuzzy little ball of lint.

Jess groaned again, louder this time. "Oh my God! Seriously?"

Jake grinned, taking it all in stride. "No prob, dudes and dudette. My dad gave me a credit card for emergencies. I'm officially declaring this an emergency."

DARKNESS HAD settled over the landscape, broken only by our headlights and the bright stars twinkling above. The moon was a yellow grin, barely visible through the trees on the horizon. We had the highway to ourselves. Only two vehicles had passed us in the past fifteen minutes, heading west, and the twin red eyes of their taillights had long since disappeared into the night.

The four of us weren't talking much. Our phones were off now, except for Toff's. He kept his on in case his dad called. So far, all he'd gotten was a call from Jessica's mom and two from my dad. They left voicemails wondering if Toff had seen either of us. Jake's parents had been ringing his phone almost nonstop. The radio couldn't pick up either a satellite signal or a local station, so the only music we had was the rush of tires over asphalt. We'd passed through the town of Selmer, Tennessee. Our destination was coming up.

Toff moved closer, pressing his shoulder against me, seeking shelter.

The headlights flashed over a green traffic sign. "There it is," Jake said quietly. "Route 28Z."

Toff sat up, his neck straining as he looked around. There wasn't much to see. No other car was in sight, nor were there any buildings, just sprawling, open plain. Route 28Z met the highway in a T, so there was only one direction Mr. Toffler could have gone. Jake slowed the car and turned south.

I kept glancing at the dashboard, counting off miles. In roughly ten minutes, we covered three miles and the terrain never changed. Not a house, barn, shed, or even a fenced-in herd of sleeping cows came in sight. "Anybody have a clue what's down this road?" I asked.

"I checked when I was on MapQuest earlier," Jessica said. "This leads to the north entrance of the Zitkala Forest Preserve. That's where the Z comes from in 28Z."

"Maybe Dad came out here to fish," said Toff, but I could tell he didn't believe that himself.

"I doubt it," said Jess. "The preserve's been closed to the public for years now."

We rode on. Within minutes the dark of night deepened around us as trees closed in on either side of the road. We must have reached the fringes of the forest preserve. Aside from the sounds of the car, dead silence surrounded us.

Jake cleared his throat. "Isn't this usually the point in a horror movie where a zombie in a hockey mask jumps out, grabs one of the teenagers, drags him into the woods, and makes sushi out of him?"

"Not helping, dude," I said between my teeth. "Try the radio again. See if we can get some music or something."

Jake tried the controls on the steering wheel, flipping from satellite to FM to AM, rolling through various channels. The screen on the radio stubbornly displayed a "no signal" message. "I'll just plug in my phone. We can listen to music that way." Keeping one hand on the wheel, he coaxed his phone from his pocket and passed it to Jess. "Would you do the honors?"

Jess thumbed the screen, which bathed her face in white light. "You don't have a signal on your phone." She got out her own cell phone. "Neither do I."

Toff and I checked our phones. "We can't get signals either," I announced.

"Maybe we're in an alternate dimension," Jess suggested. "You know, like something out of a Stephen King story. Maybe we're on the road to hell."

"Maybe you could shut the hell up," I replied, again through my clenched teeth.

"Jess, I think the dude is scared," Jake said with a laugh.

"Aww, are you afraid, La Forge?"

"Yeah, Jess. I'm afraid I'm gonna choke you and Jake if you don't zip your lips."

The three of us bantered back and forth that way for a while. It helped ease the tension a little, at least for me. Toff kept quiet. I could sense how jumpy he was. I squeezed his hand; it felt cold yet sweaty. "You okay?" I whispered.

He nodded and then put his head on my shoulder, snuggling against me. I kissed his forehead. "Everything's gonna be fine with your dad, man. You'll see." It didn't feel strange or wrong to comfort and reassure him. I would have gladly given him anything he needed.

The road narrowed to one lane in either direction. Shortly after that the asphalt gave way to gravel.

"What's that up ahead?" said Jessica.

About five hundred feet or so away, the road ended. A closed and latched gate, bristling with thick metal locks, awaited us there. As Jess had said, a sign on the gate warned that the preserve was closed to the public.

Jess pointed out the sign and then looked around at the rest of us. "What do we do now? Go back?"

"Wait! Look." Toff pointed anxiously.

It was difficult to see anything at first. Then, as we got closer, the beams from the headlights fell on the edge of some bulky object partially hidden behind a tree off to one side of the road. Jake applied the brakes. As he pulled to a stop beside the object, I saw that it was a car.

Mr. Toffler's car.

CHAPTER 12

THE BROWN Camry looked ghostly, blending into the deep shadows beneath the trees. The driver's window was down. Toff stuck his head in, looked around, then pulled out, turned, and yelled, "Dad!" into the forest. The anxious wail of his voice bounced off the trees, echoing eerily back at us. The echo faded, leaving us with the stark silence of the woods.

I opened the driver's door and peered into the cabin. Plastic bags, cardboard tags, and cash register receipts were scattered over the seat and floorboard of the front passenger side. In the back seat were scattered articles of clothing—a pair of jeans, a sneaker, a green camouflage baseball cap, the one I'd seen Mr. Toffler wearing since spring.

"Hey, guys," Jess said, her voice hushed with apprehension. "The trunk's open."

I pulled out of the cabin and hurried after the others. We gathered round the back of the car. The lid of the trunk was up a few inches, exposing a swath of the blackness within. None of us moved for a moment, and I was sure the others were experiencing the same foreboding sense of I-don't-want-to-see-what's-in-here.

Jess reached out and lifted the lid.

I exhaled, a near-silent sigh of relief. The trunk was stuffed with luggage. A couple of the pieces were unzipped, clothes hanging out of one duffel bag while the other was nearly empty. Toff dug through the trunk and came up with a green, accordion-style portable file. He opened it and named off the contents as he leafed through them. "My parents' marriage license... my mom's death certificate... the deed to our house... living will... my birth certificate...."

"Why would your dad bring important papers like that out here?" Jake asked.

"And he just left them," Jess added. "He didn't even bother to make sure the trunk was locked."

"Dad!" Toff called out again, his voice louder and more plaintive.

"I don't like this," Jess said. "We should call the police."

"How?" I asked. "None of our phones work out here."

"The last time I had a signal was when we were in Selmer," Jake said. "We should head back that way."

"We can't just leave," Toff snapped. "We have to find my dad."

"How do we even begin to search?" asked Jess. "We don't know which direction he went. If we go back to Selmer and call the police—"

"I'm not leaving," said Toff. "I'm not leaving until I find my dad."

Toff stuffed the file back in the trunk and slammed down the lid. He turned, scanning the woods with his eyes. He was dead serious about not leaving. I could see it in the way his face was set.

"Jake, take Jess, drive back to Selmer, and get the police," I said. "I'll stay with Toff."

"Are you out of your mind?" Jess looked ready to grab my shoulders and shake me. "We're not leaving you guys out here roaming around in these woods."

"We'll be okay," I said, although I was feeling pretty skeptical about that.

"Jess is right," said Jake. "If we leave you, we'll wind up with three missing people instead of one. How about this? What say we search the forest together as a group—no splitting up—to see if we can pick up a trail or something on Toff's dad? We give it an hour, and if we don't find anything, we drive out of here and call the cops."

"That's dumb," Jess said bluntly. "It's dark as hell in those woods. How would we find our way back to the car? We'll all wind up lost out there."

"My mom keeps an emergency kit in her trunk," Jake said. "It has a flashlight, flares, a compass and a lot of other stuff. We won't get lost."

Jessica put her hands on her hips. "And you guarantee that on your good looks?"

Jake hesitated only a moment. "Well... no, I can't guarantee anything. I'm not *that* good-looking."

Jessica scowled at him. I thought she was going to cuss him in Spanish and English, a two-for-the-price-of-one deal. Then her eyebrows went up in admiration. "Damn. You really are honest."

"Yep. Honest. Heroic. Hot. Handsome." Jake, flashing a devastatingly winsome smile, winked at Jess. "And I'm modest too."

"HEY! HERE'S a trail."

Jake, Jess, and I hurried to where Toff stood waving us over. The four of us had been scouting around the north entrance of the forest preserve, looking for a clue as to the direction Mr. Toffler had taken. A trail through the woods certainly qualified. Toff knelt, studying the ground before him. "Let me have the flashlight," he said.

Jake handed him the light. Toff trained the beam on the ground. "Look!" Toff said. "Footprints. They're my dad's."

I let my eyes follow the yellow circle of light as Toff moved it along the narrow dirt trail, illuminating the set of prints he'd found. They were sort of big, and I suppose that made them masculine, but I didn't get the connection Toff had made. "Man, what makes you think these are your dad's prints? They could be anybody's."

"No, Geordi. I know my dad's work boots. The sole of his boots leaves prints just like these. And these prints are fresh. These have to be my dad's."

There was another print on the trail, at the edge of the circle of illumination cast down by the flashlight. That print had been made by a sneaker, and it was older than the boot prints; pine needles and twigs had been scattered across it. But Toff was sure about the boot prints. I looked at Jess and Jake. Jake shrugged in a don't-ask-me way. "Hey, it's as good a direction as any," Jess said.

Toff took the lead with the light. Jake fell in close behind him. I let Jess go ahead and brought up the rear. The trail was narrow enough that we were forced to walk it single file. The trees were mostly pine, growing close together, and the darkness filling the gaps between was as thick and impenetrable as a curtain. Cricket love songs and the hoots of owls filled the air, but it was the absence of human sounds—car doors slamming, laughter, music, chatter—that made the night close in on us like a hungry thing. I felt small and afraid, like a little boy who'd lost his parents.

"SO TOFF, why'd your dad do this?" Jake asked. "Why'd he come out here, in the middle of nowhere, to a forest nobody is supposed to come to?"

Toff sighed. He sounded tired and sad. "I don't know, Jake. I don't know why my dad ever does any of the stuff he does. I don't even know why he gets up in the morning. He's never happy or sad. He never seems to enjoy anything…." He made a quick, dismissive brushing motion with his hand. "Sorry. I shouldn't go off like that."

"It's okay by me," said Jake. "Sometimes you just have to get things off your chest."

Toff and Jake were walking close together. I thought they needed a little space, and Jess seemed to agree. We hung back about twenty or thirty feet, which was the maximum distance we could allow without losing the guiding illumination of the flashlight Toff carried. We hadn't seen any boot prints in a while, probably because of all the brown pine needles scattered over the ground, and now were simply following the trail. The four of us were nearing the end of the hour we'd allotted ourselves for the search. We would have to turn back soon, whether we found anything or not.

I watched Toff and Jake as they continued their conversation. They seemed comfortable together, as if they had known each other for years.

Yeah. Comfortable. For years.

Jess leaned close to me and whispered, "Jealous?"

What the hell? "Of who?"

She nodded toward Toff and Jake.

"No," I whispered. "That's crazy. Why in the world would I be jealous of them?"

Jess pressed her lips together in a smug expression that nearly drove me insane. "If you're not jealous, then you're awfully pissed at them. You're staring them down like you're gonna snort fire from your nose."

I crossed my eyes at her, my way of letting her know I thought her sanity had gone off the rails. She was right about the anger, though. I hadn't been aware of what I was feeling until she mentioned it. Suddenly, I wished more than anything that Toff and Jake had never met. None of those feelings made sense to me. I hated when my own heart and head were a mystery to me.

"So what crawled up your tailpipe?" Jess said. "Seriously. You've been sour ever since you showed up with your face punched out. Is that it? You angry with the person who hit you?"

"Carson kicked my ass, but I blame my dad for it."

"Well, don't stop there. I can't wait to hear how Carson punching you out was your dad's fault."

"Dad put pictures of Carson, Toff, and me on Facebook with this big-ass headline about having everybody meet my new boyfriend. Carson's dad saw the picture, which made it look like Carson and I were the boyfriends, and he gave Carson hell. So Carson gave me hell. And I got mad at my dad. I... told him that I hate him."

Jess let loose with a swat on my arm. "Geordi!"

"I'm not good at telling people how I really feel."

"That wasn't saying how you really feel. That was disrespectful. There's a difference. You owe your dad an apology."

I already knew that. To keep from getting angry with myself, I tuned back into the conversation between Toff and Jake.

"Where's your mom?" Jake asked.

"Dead," Toff replied quietly.

"Oh. Sorry."

"I wish I could have known her. She died when I was two. It's a strange thing to say, considering I don't even remember what her voice sounded like, but I miss her."

"There's nothing strange about that." Jake fell silent for a moment. When he spoke again, his voice was softer, and cautious. "Maybe that's what happened to your dad. Maybe your mom's death changed him."

"Changed him from what? The way he is now is the only way I've ever known him to be."

"But he could've been different with your mom. Like, happy and full of life."

Toff abruptly stopped walking, forcing Jake to an awkward halt to avoid colliding with him. He turned to Jake. "You think... my dad still misses her too?"

"Sure. Why not? I mean... she was his wife."

Jess and I caught up to them. Toff looked as if he were about to throw up or something. "I don't think the way he is now comes from just missing my mom," he said, shifting his gaze from Jake to Jess to me. "When Dad buried my mom, he buried every part of himself with her. He never gave a damn about me or anything else because he put every piece of his heart in the ground with her."

He held my gaze, waiting, a plea burning in his face. What was I supposed to say to that? The only thing I could think of was to hold him, to offer him fresh assurances that he would get through this awful part of his life. Before I could reach for him, however, Jess grabbed my wrist tightly. "Guys," she hissed, pointing with her other hand, "what's that?"

In the immediate area ahead of us, not more than ten feet away, the pale haze from the flashlight reflected off a pair of large green eyes that stared at us out of the darkness. The hair rose on the back of my neck. We were being watched by a monster, one that was no doubt giving thanks that its evening meal had just walked up and served itself in four courses. I probably would have screamed, fainted, or pissed myself if Jess hadn't gone charging forward, waving her arms like crazy. "Hyah!" she shouted.

The monster took off in an impressive display of wide, flapping wings, warbling a series of angry hoots at us as it swept overhead and disappeared into the dark treetops.

"Okay!" I heaved in relief. "I need a fresh pair of shorts. Anybody else?"

Jake chuckled nervously and shook his head, providing the only laugh I could get from my friends. Toff pressed forward, skimming the darkness ahead with the flashlight's beam. "Hey," he called out. "I think the trail ends here."

Jess, Jake, and I walked over to join Toff where he stood at the edge of the woods. The trail didn't actually end there. It ran across the wide clearing before us down to the grassy bank of a lake. The lake stretched out for a mile or more, bordered on its opposite bank by a dark mass of trees. Its waters were black and flat under the openness of the starry sky. If a man wanted to lose himself in the lazy peace of a day of fishing, this was definitely the spot.

With the starlight unhindered by leafy treetops, the darkness here didn't seem as oppressive as in the woods. The four of us stood looking out over the lake, taking in the area. To the north, a wooden pier extended several feet over the water, ending in a large gazebo from which lines could be dangled while fishermen took their ease in the shade. Mr. Toffler might be under that gazebo. Maybe it was just me, but sleeping on a wooden bench under an actual roof seemed better than lying on the ground under a tree.

A tinny beep floated across the air, barely audible over the chirping sounds of the crickets. We looked at each other, surprised and puzzled. The beep repeated itself in a steady rhythm. It was the kind of noise that came from an electronic device, a laptop or something. Actually, it reminded me of the timer on the stove in my parents' kitchen. We turned, our eyes darting this way and that, trying to pinpoint the source. I looked at the gazebo again.

Yup. The beeps were definitely coming from the gazebo.

I got the others' attention, pointed at the gazebo, put a finger to my lips for their silence, and motioned for them to follow. I was pretty sure that we'd found Mr. Toffler—the beeps were probably coming from his watch—and that he was asleep in the gazebo. Mr. Toffler owned a gun, and according to Toff, he'd taken the gun with him when he left home. I didn't want to startle a man with a gun.

The beeping grew louder as we got closer to the gazebo. The structure was plain, lacking any ornamentation such as lattice work or arches. Even in the darkness, I could see how weathered the wood was, worn gray and smooth from decades of exposure to the elements. The gazebo was octagonal in shape, with a wooden bench built into the rail on each of its eight sides.

Someone was lying on one of those benches.

The four of us spotted the person at the same time. A sort of collective pause went through us as we each came to an uncertain stop. The guy was asleep; his snores were so slight they were barely audible over the steady beeping. And I recognized the pattern of the beeps now. That was the alert Mr. Toffler programmed on his cell phone to let him know when the battery needed a recharge.

On a silent agreement made through an exchange of uneasy looks, we moved slowly and quietly around the south-facing side of the gazebo to the north side where the sleeping man lay on his back with one leg drooping off the bench and one arm flung over his face. A smell hung over him like a fog, the scent of a several-day accumulation of sweat, not quite strong enough to bring tears to the eyes but getting there.

Peering over the rail, the first thing I noticed was that the man wore a Baltimore Orioles T-shirt with a rip in the left sleeve. Toff had accidentally made that tear one day when he borrowed the shirt from his dad's dresser drawer. Then I noticed Mr. Toffler's leather-banded watch on the man's wrist, which was close to his right ear. Mr. Toffler's cell phone lay on his chest, still in the green camouflage case Toff had given his dad last year as a birthday present. And the boots the man wore were indeed one of the three pairs Mr. Toffler had used for his construction job.

The only problem was that the man bearing all those things wasn't Mr. Toffler.

Toff reacted the way most people would under such circumstances. He barked out a loud, angry "Hey!" Startled, the guy flipped off the bench in a flurry of flailing limbs, sending the cell phone clattering to the floor of the gazebo. He was on his feet, backing away from us, his left hand held out as if to keep us at bay. His right hand had been slipped into the pocket of his dirty and tattered jeans. He was tall, thin, and only a few years older than us—maybe eighteen or nineteen. His long blond hair was pulled back and tied in a ponytail at the nape of his neck. His expression was wild with surprise, fear, and maybe just a hint of instability. My brain flashed danger signals with every pulse of adrenaline that went through my body.

Toff was too outraged to heed any such signals. He climbed quickly over the rail and scooped up the fallen cell phone. He never took his eyes off the blond guy as he advanced slowly toward him. "That's my dad's stuff," he snarled. "That's his shirt, his watch"—he held out the phone toward the guy—"his cell phone… his boots!"

With his left arm still extended, the guy shook his head vigorously. He wasn't doing that in denial; he didn't understand what Toff was talking about. I could see that in the guy's face. He backed cautiously away.

I didn't like the way he kept his right hand in his pocket.

"What did you do to him?" Toff dropped the cell phone as he kept moving slowly forward. His hands clenched into fists. "Where is he? Where's my dad?"

Jess started to climb over the rail. I grabbed her arm, pulled her back. I shook my head at her and at Jake, hoping telepathy would convey the warning in my head: *Stay back. No sudden moves. Don't scare the guy.*

Toff was doing a pretty good job of that already. Although the guy was older and several inches taller, Toff was so upset I figured he could inflict some serious injury if he got his hands on Blondie. I was also worried about what the blond guy might do to Toff if he brought that right hand out of his pocket.

"Toff!" I hissed. "Stop. Don't walk up on him."

Toff either didn't hear me or didn't give a damn about what I was saying. He kept advancing, one slow, menacing step after the other. The guy backed up against the rail on the opposite side of the gazebo. He shook his head again.

"You have his stuff, my dad's stuff," Toff said. His arms were shaking now from his rage. "Tell me where he is!"

Toff lunged. I moved instinctively, pulling myself up. As I leaped over the rail, I saw the blond guy whip his right hand out of his pocket. He brought the gun up in a fluid motion so fast it stopped Toff and me before either of us could reach him.

His face scrunched in panic, his arm trembling, the guy held the gun with his finger on the trigger. The barrel was aimed at Toff's face.

CHAPTER 13

I'D NEVER seen Mr. Toffler's gun, but I was sure it was the same one the blond guy now held on Toff. The irony of my best friend taking a bullet from his own dad's firearm wasn't lost on me. I was afraid for all of us, even the guy with the weapon, who appeared more desperate to escape than intent on doing harm. Somehow, desperation made him more dangerous in my mind.

With the gun on him, Toff had stopped advancing momentarily, but he still looked anguished. He wanted answers from this guy, and he looked as if he wasn't going to let a little thing like a bullet stop him from getting them. When I saw him edge one foot forward again, I did something extremely stupid.

"Hey, hey," I said, easing myself between Toff and Blondie with my hands raised like a character in an old Western movie. The dude shifted his gaze to me but kept the gun on Toff. "We don't want to hurt you or anything. My friend here is trying to find his dad. You have some of his dad's clothes and stuff. We just want to know where you got them, that's all."

The guy didn't say anything. His breathing was heavy and fast. He shifted his eyes rapidly all over the place, from me to Toff to somewhere in back of us. I couldn't see Jess or Jake, but I hoped to heaven they weren't planning to bum-rush the guy or anything. We couldn't all afford to go stupid.

"Hey," I said, a little louder this time. I was trying to recapture the guy's focus. His eyes kept flitting nervously around. "Everything's cool, okay. Nobody's gonna hurt you. Put the gun down and we'll talk. That's all we want. Put the gun down."

Finally, he locked eyes with me. Honestly, he looked too scared to actually shoot someone. For a while it seemed as if he would actually lower the gun. Then he said in a high, scratchy voice, "You think I'm crazy. I'm *not* crazy." His eyes narrowed as he swiveled the gun toward me.

Everything went black.

I THOUGHT I was dead.

Death was a frantic state. In the eternal blackness, there was a whole lot of motion and noise.

Something whizzed past my face. Did I still have a face? A muffled *crack* burrowed through the darkness. Someone yelped, a sharp cry of pain. Something big shot past me on the left. A meaty thump followed, then a loud grunt. Only a second later, something moved on my right, brushing past my arm. Did I still have an arm? The darkness itself seemed to shift and jerk in front of me.

"Geordi!"

I opened my eyes.

I was still standing. There was no bullet hole in my forehead, or any other part of my body.

At my feet, Toff and Jake were struggling to hold the blond guy on the floor of the gazebo as Jess tried to pry the gun from his hand. Blondie was fighting like crazy to break away. And he was winning. Toff was trying to pin his legs but couldn't get a solid grip on the wildly kicking limbs. Jake took a punch on the side of his head that appeared to daze him for a moment, causing his arms to loosen their grip around the guy's torso. Jess looked up at me as she slammed the guy's gun hand against one of the rails. "A little help here!" she snapped.

I lurched forward and Blondie kicked me in the chest with one of those heavy, steel-toed work boots. It felt as if my lungs had exploded. I gulped hollowly, unable to take in a breath, and stumbled backward into one of the gazebo's support posts. My head bumped against the post, and I got a flash of stars to go along with the pain bouncing around in my chest. I struggled to inhale.

Jess slammed the guy's arm against the rail again, and the gun flew out of his hand and over the side. There was a solid splash as it hit the water and sank. With the gun out of the way, Jess drew back and landed a quick jab on Blondie's already crooked nose. Blood spurted from his nostrils, but that didn't take the fight out of him. He kept kicking at Toff, and one of his boots grazed the side of Toff's head. Toff fell on his back, bumping forcefully against Jess's legs and taking her down as well.

That only left Jake. It was obvious he didn't want to throw punches if he didn't have to. On his knees, he tried to wrestle the dude down and pin him. The guy slammed him in the shoulders, forcing him back enough that Jake couldn't grab him again. Blondie scrambled to his feet.

"Look, man, we don't have to fight anymore," Jake said. "Just calm down and we can—"

Blondie yelled something unintelligible and threw himself over the rail into the lake, sending a spray of water high in the air. He splashed wildly as he swam along the side of the gazebo and crawled up onto the bank. Once he got his feet under him again, he broke into a frantic dash, heading into the woods. Toff started to rush across the gazebo and go after him. Jess and I both grabbed him. "Let the guy go," Jess said.

"He did something to my dad!" Toff shouted, staring after him, fighting to pull away. "We can't let him get away!"

"We can't chase him through the woods, Toff," I said, watching as Blondie vanished in the darkness among the trees. "We don't know what's out there, and it's time to get the police involved—"

"*No!*" Toff spun around, shouting in my face with more anguish than I'd ever seen in another human being.

Jess stepped closer, towering over the both of us, and gave Toff's shoulder a soft, reassuring squeeze. "That guy is dangerous, Toff. He pulled a gun on us, and he probably would have shot Geordi if Jake hadn't knocked his arm down. We're going back to the car, Jake's gonna drive us to Selmer, and we're calling the police."

Toff mumbled something under his breath and shook his head, still protesting. Jessica got right in his face and said firmly, "Come on. Let's go."

Jake retrieved the flashlight and the compass, which had been dropped during all the scuffling. I wrapped Toff in a hug, offering what little comfort I could. Jess gave his shoulder another squeeze. We made our way back to the trail, and Jake led the way through the woods at a pretty fast clip.

It took maybe half an hour for us to reach the north entrance of the forest preserve. "Wait," Toff said. He went immediately to his dad's car, reached through the open driver's window, and pressed the trunk release button. He went to the back of the car, lifted the lid, retrieved the portable file, and closed the lid again. "I'm ready now," he announced.

Toff and I climbed into the back seat of Jake's mom's car, and he carefully tucked the file between us. Jake and Jessica slid in the front, and Jake started the engine. He wasn't moving fast enough for me. I'd had enough of dark woods and abandoned cars and smelly guys with guns. I'm not a particularly religious guy, but when Jake put the car in gear, circled the clearing, and started back up Route 28Z, I breathed a short, silent prayer of thanks.

THE NIGHT was clear and peaceful, and ours was the only car on the road as far as we could see. None of us spoke on the long drive down Highway 64. Our phones were turned on again, and periodically one of us would check to see if there was a signal. When we hit the five-mile marker outside of Selmer, all four of us jumped at the sudden, heavy sound of big knuckles knocking hard on wood—Jess's new ringtone. She lifted the phone and checked the caller ID. "It's my brother, Javier," she said. "I'm gonna let that go to voicemail. Jake, pull over at the next gas station."

Five minutes later we rolled into the lot of a Shell station. Jake pulled into a parking slot in front of the convenience store and shut off the engine. "Okay, now what?" he asked.

"Now that we have a signal, Geordi, Toff, and I are gonna get out here," Jess answered. "And you, *mi amigo*, had better hightail it home."

"I don't want to just leave you guys here," Jake protested.

"I'm about to make a call to the police," Jess said. "You don't want them tagging you for driving without a license, so just go on home. I'm calling my mom after I call the police. We'll be okay."

Jake looked back at Toff and me, uncertainty and reluctance in his eyes. "We'll see you later, man," I said, and opened the door. I paused with one foot on the asphalt when Toff said, "Jake?"

"Yeah, man?"

"Take this with you," Toff said, patting the top of the portable file. "I don't want the cops to take it. Hide it in your room or something, and I'll get it from you later."

"You got it."

Jess, Toff, and I climbed out. We sent Jake off with our thanks and our goodbyes, and I watched as the car grew smaller and smaller until it disappeared over a hill down the highway.

Jess blew out a breath. "Okay. Let's get this over with." She lifted her phone and dialed 911, and I felt more dread than I had when we were deep in the forest. She put her phone on speaker.

"Nine one one, what is your emergency?"

"My name is Jessica Sanchez, and I want to report that my friend's father is missing, and that a man with a gun just got into a fight with me and my friends."

"Where's the man with the gun?"

"He ran off into the woods."

"Are you and your friends safe?"

"Yes. We just need to get the police out here."

"Where are you?"

"We're at the Shell station off the westbound side of Highway 64, about four and a half miles east of Selmer."

"How old are you, Jessica?"

"I'm fourteen."

"Is there an adult with you?"

"No. I'm calling my mom as soon as I finish talking to you."

"All right. Stay there. The sheriff is on the way."

Jess disconnected the call. She looked nervously at Toff and me. "Now comes the *really* fun part." She thumbed a number on her phone. Her call was answered quickly. "Hi, Mom," she said, lowering her eyes contritely. "No, I'm okay. I'm with Toff and Geordi...."

Jess shifted into Spanish. I nudged Toff with my shoulder and nodded toward the convenience store. He followed me over to the front of the store where we sat down on the ground with our backs to the wall. I started to ask if he was okay, but that would have been stupid. He was far from okay. His body was trembling. You could see right off how upset he was. The only thing I could do was be there for him. I put my arm around his shoulders while Jess went on talking with her mom.

After a few minutes, Jessica's voice got loud, drawing a concerned look from Toff. She rolled her eyes hard, murmured something that sounded like an apology, and lowered her voice. When she disconnected the call moments later, she let her head fall back and groaned. Toff and I started to get up and go to her, but she waved and we settled back against the wall. She walked over and sat down next to Toff.

"So what did your mom say?" Toff asked.

"She and Javier are on their way. I told her that, by the time they get here, we'll most likely be at the north entrance of the forest preserve with the sheriff. She said the sheriff will just have to arrest her because she's going to pin me up by my ears to the nearest tree. Oh, and Geordi, she told me to tell you to be sure to have your phone turned on. Your mom and dad have called her a couple of times trying to track you down. She said they were pretty upset, and she's giving them a call to let them know where you are."

"Cripes, Jess," I snapped. "Did you just *have* to tell your mom I'm out here with you?"

She shrugged casually at me. "Why should I be the only one pinned up to a tree by a parent?"

Bells jingled. I turned to see the clerk pushing open the door of the convenience store. A twenty-something woman in blue jeans and a white smock, she leaned out the doorway, looking curiously at us. "Is everything all right with you guys?" she asked.

"We're dead," I replied flatly.

Which got me a swat in the back of the head from Jess. "Ow!"

Jess beamed at the clerk. "Everything's just fine."

SHERIFF ELAINE Villanova was a small middle-aged African American woman with auburn hair worn in a pixie cut, all of five feet three inches tall (I'm being generous there). She had big dark Bambi eyes and cheeks that dimpled when she smiled. Which she did only once, when she arrived at the Shell station with three deputies in tow and introduced herself to us. Her deputies, all men, were taller and stronger and meaner-looking, but there was never any doubt as to who was in charge. In her gray uniform and black boots, with her badge on her chest and her gun on her hip, the sheriff was pretty damn intimidating.

We were at the north entrance of the forest preserve again, the three deputies were off in the woods looking for Blondie and Mr. Toffler, and Sheriff Villanova was glaring up at Jessica in a way that made me so nervous my throat went dry. "You want to run that by me again?" the sheriff huffed.

"Sure," Jess replied innocently. "We hitched our way out here."

"The three of you hitched a two-hundred-mile ride from Memphis?"

"Yes, ma'am."

"Who'd you hitch the ride with?"

"She said her name is Sam."

"A woman named Sam."

"Yeah. It must be short for Samsara or Samuelita or something. She didn't give her last name."

"Of course not. And you don't have her phone number either."

"No, we didn't get that."

"Uh-huh." The sheriff hitched up her pants on one side. "So this generous no-last-name woman, whose phone number you don't have, drove you three all the way out here to look for this boy's father." She pointed at Toff. "How did you get from here to the Shell station?"

"Sam waited right here for us, and then she drove us to the gas station."

"This woman Sam with no last name and no phone number, sat out in the middle of nowhere for an hour or more, while you three kids went off in the woods and got yourselves attacked by a guy with a gun, and then she drove you to a gas station, dropped you off, and disappeared into the night, never to be seen nor heard from again."

"Yeah, that's it. You're exactly right."

Sheriff Villanova folded her arms across her chest. "Jessica Sanchez, do you realize it is a crime to lie to an officer of the law?"

Jess nodded solemnly. "Of course. And I would never, ever lie to a cop."

The sheriff looked at me. I smiled at her. It was one of those I'm-guilty-as-heck-but please-don't-lock-me-up smiles. The sheriff sniffed in a disgusted sort of way and turned to Toff. "Sandor, when was the last time you spoke to your dad?"

"That was Sunday," said Toff. "He told me he was going off to fish at Shelby Farms. After that he never answered any of my calls or texts."

"He never said anything about coming here?"

"No."

"And you have no idea why he would come to this forest preserve?"

"No."

The sheriff didn't look as if she believed Toff any more than she believed Jessica. She also was starting to look pissed, probably because of her suspicion that she was being lied to. I felt a little relieved when the glare of headlights flashed over us, followed by the hum of multiple car engines. Two vehicles rumbled their way toward us along Route 28Z. Although the darkness obscured details of the approaching cars, I was pretty sure who was coming, and my relief only lasted a couple of seconds.

The cars stopped behind the three patrol cars bearing the logo of the McNairy County Sheriff's Department. The doors on the lead car opened, and Mrs. Sanchez and Javier climbed out. My mom and dad came rushing out of the second car. The four of them hurried over to where Toff, Jess, and I stood with the sheriff. Javier, around six foot four and pole-like with a mass of black curls on his head, was usually one big pile of snark. He teased Jess, Toff, me, and her other friends whenever he was around, which thankfully wasn't often. Like Carson, he was usually a Class A asshole. Tonight, he looked as if he'd shrunk an inch or two, subdued perhaps by the sheer craziness that had brought us all out here. He moved in close to Jess, hovering protectively over her.

Mrs. Sanchez shot a quick and very angry look at Jess as she extended her hand to the sheriff. "Hello. I'm Mara Sanchez, Jessica's mother. This is my son, Javier."

"And we're the Quintrells, Ben and Diana," Dad said, offering his hand after the sheriff finished shaking with Jess's mom. "We're Geordi's parents."

"You're all from Memphis, I take it," said the sheriff after introducing herself.

"Yes," said Mom. "Have you found Sandor's father?"

"I still have three of my men out searching. It may be a while before we know anything about him." The sheriff threw another annoyed glance at Jess, Toff, and me. "But I've interviewed the kids, and here's what I know so far from them. They went to the missing man's job and were told he was last seen at Highway 64 and Route 28Z. They hitchhiked their way here with a woman none of them knows, found the missing man's car abandoned, went into the forest to look for him, and got attacked by another man who was wearing some of the missing man's clothes. That man pulled a gun on them."

"A gun?" Mom, Dad, and Mrs. Sanchez all barked in horrified unison.

"Yes. They said they fought the man and managed to knock the gun out of his hand into some lake, and the man ran off into the forest. We're trying to track this man down as well."

With equal portions of fear and fury on her face, her mouth hanging open, Mrs. Sanchez turned to glare at Jessica. I lowered my eyes to the ground so I wouldn't have to see the way my parents looked at me. Toff took my hand and squeezed.

"Folks," Sheriff Villanova said, "this is an active crime scene. I'm going to have to ask you all to leave now so we can process the scene and continue our investigation. I understand you'll be returning to Memphis—"

"I don't want to go back yet," Toff interrupted. He looked anxiously from Mrs. Sanchez to my parents. "I want to stay until they find my dad."

I turned to Mom. "Can't we stay, you, me, and Toff? Can't we get a room at a motel somewhere?"

"That is something to consider, Mrs. Sanchez, Mr. and Mrs. Quintrell," said the sheriff. "At some point I will need to talk with the kids again. If you stay somewhere locally, it will save you from having to drive back from Memphis."

"Sheriff, my son and I have to work tomorrow," Mrs. Sanchez said. "We'll have to go home tonight. But I will arrange to get Jessica back here when you need to talk with her. And believe me, she will fully cooperate with you in every way." She said that last sentence while shooting lasers from her eyes at Jess. Things were not going to be pretty in the Sanchez home tonight.

Dad was looking at me, but I avoided looking back at him. "My wife and I will stay here tonight with the boys," he said to the sheriff.

Mom raised her eyebrows in surprise. "We will?"

"We'll find a hotel in Selmer," Dad went on, "and stay at least through tomorrow."

"All right. Let me get everyone's phone numbers and home addresses, and then you folks can be on your way." Sheriff Villanova pulled out a pad and pen.

CHAPTER 14

WE STOPPED at a Walmart where Mom and Dad bought toothpaste, toothbrushes, deodorant, a change of underwear for each of us, and a nightie for Mom. Then we got two rooms at Miranda's Bed and Breakfast on the outskirts of Selmer's business district. It was twenty minutes until midnight. I felt tired and achy all the way down to my bones. I could see that Toff felt the same, on top of all the fear and worry he felt for his father. When Dad handed me the card key to the room I'd be sharing with Toff, I wanted nothing more than a quick shower, some time to comfort Toff, and then my head on a pillow.

With the door pushed open, I walked into the room, followed by Toff. The room looked cozy and homey. There were two full-sized beds with what appeared to be handmade quilts, two padded rocking chairs beside a fireplace, a shelf lined with books, and two recliners facing a television. I was on a beeline to the attached bathroom when Dad said, "Okay, Diana, I know you're not comfortable with the boys bunking together now, so I'll stay in here with them."

I stopped right at the bathroom door. *Oh. Hell. No.* There was no way I'd room with Dad. I'd sleep naked on the roof before I'd let that happen.

"No, you don't have to do that, Ben," said Mom. "Why don't you take Toff over to our room for a while? I want to have a talk with Geordi."

Dad walked over and put a hand on Toff's shoulder. His hand looked massive and strong. He stood a solid six feet. I wondered, not for the first time, if I'd ever have his height and his strength. I wondered when I'd be able to get away from him for good. "Come on, kiddo," Dad said as he began to escort Toff out of the room. "You look as if you have a lot on your mind. Maybe you and I can have our own talk."

Mom closed the door after them, still holding the Walmart bag with the things she'd purchased for herself. "Let's sit down, Geordi," she said, gesturing toward the rocking chairs.

We sat down with our bodies angled toward each other. Mom placed the bag on her lap. The fireplace between us added an air of intimacy that seemed to pull us even closer together. Mom had every reason to be royally pissed with me, but I didn't sense any anger in her. She reached over and tenderly took my hand.

"Honey," she said, "you are so in love with Toff."

No. I'm not.

"I see that. You've been in love with him for a good while, and I'm surprised the two of you didn't get together before now. I understand how your feelings for him can make you want to stand by him. That's one of the beautiful things about love, the way it makes us take care of each other. But Geordi, you can't let love blind you to certain realities."

"What realities, Mom?"

"That the two of you are still children, for one thing. Sure, you're old enough to make certain decisions for yourselves, old enough to have sex—"

"Toff and I aren't having sex. I don't think we'll ever have sex."

She smiled. It was one of those yeah-right smiles. "Just let me finish. The two of you are only a few years away from being adults, but you're not there yet, and some things you have to leave to adults. You, Toff, and Jess never should have tried to find Mr. Toffler on your own. Once he disappeared you kids should have come to me or your dad or Mrs. Sanchez. You should have let us deal with it."

"But Toff didn't want me or Jess to tell anybody. He was so upset and so scared, and I didn't want to make things worse for him."

"How much worse would things have been if you or he or Jess had gotten shot trying to find his dad?"

Oh. Good point.

"I don't believe for one second the three of you hitchhiked your way out here. Someone you know brought you, and you don't want to say who that was. Is that person safe?"

"Uhm… yeah. Definitely." Jake had sent me a text message after he pulled his mom's car into the garage. He said it would probably be the last text I got from him for a while. I'm sure there was a serious grounding in his immediate future. Just as there was about to be in mine.

"Okay. Then that's an issue we can leave until another time. You, Toff, and Jessica had no idea what you were getting yourselves into.

What you did was very dangerous, even for an adult. That's why we have the police, to deal with situations like this. And did you stop to think for one moment how frantic Mrs. Sanchez, your dad, and I would be if you kids disappeared for hours, at night, with your cell phones shut off?"

"I know, Mom, and I'm sorry. We didn't want to worry anybody."

"But that's exactly what you did. I shake every time I think of the danger you put yourselves in… fighting a man with a gun…."

"We found Mr. Toffler's footprints on a trail going into the forest, so we followed the trail and found this guy sleeping by the lake. He had on some of Mr. Toffler's clothes, so we figured he must know where Mr. Toffler was. We were just trying to get him to tell us, but he pulled out a gun, and it was Mr. Toffler's gun. And then we were all fighting, the gun got knocked into the water, the guy ran off, and that's when Jess called the police."

Mom held my hand tighter. "Oh, Geordi. I am so glad none of you were seriously hurt. But you must never do anything like this again. Do you understand?"

"Yes, Mom."

"You know you're going to be punished for this."

I sighed in resignation. "Yes, Mom."

"Just so we're clear. Now, let's talk about you and Toff and sex."

"Mom, on that subject, there's nothing to talk about."

"Let's talk anyway. The sexual urge is in overdrive at your age. And when you're in love with someone, the desire to be intimate with him can become even stronger."

Yeah, I want to be intimate with a guy all right, just not with Toff.

"You're growing up so fast. I suppose part of me wants to keep you my little precious prince for a while longer, but I have to face certain realities as well. I understand that you and Toff want to have sex. And I know that when you feel ready for it, you're going to do it. That's natural and certainly nothing to be ashamed of or uptight about. But I want you to be safe if and when you do choose to have sex." She reached into the Walmart bag and produced a small box of condoms. "Do you know how to use one of these?"

I'd never seen an actual condom outside its packaging. I shrugged in an offhand gesture. "I guess."

"I don't want you to guess, honey. I want you to be sure. There are a number of diseases that can be transmitted sexually, such as gonorrhea, syphilis, and HIV. A condom can help protect you from those diseases." She opened the box and pulled out an individually wrapped packet, which she held up in front of me. "First of all, check the expiration date. If that date has passed, the condom is useless because it can tear or break while you're having sex. When you open this, you want to be sure you don't damage the condom." She tore the tinfoil-type packet carefully and pulled out a pale yellow, slicked down, rolled up deflated balloon. "The condom comes out like this. You don't want to unroll it before you try to put it on, and you don't want to put it on until the penis is erect. The condom goes on before your penis comes in contact with any part of your partner's body, or your partner's penis comes in contact with any part of your body. There's a tip at the end to hold the semen. This part is placed over the head of the penis. Make sure this ridge here is on the outside of the condom. If it's inside, you have the condom on the wrong way. Roll the ridge down, over the shaft, all the way to the base of the penis." She held up two fingers and demonstrated the procedure. "You should always use a water-based lubricant with condoms. I have some in the bag here. Never use lotion, petroleum jelly, or anything oily. When sex is over, always hold the base of the condom before you pull out to make sure nothing spills. Do you have any questions?"

"Well, not a question. More of an observation."

"And what is that?"

"Mom, this is the weirdest conversation I've ever had with you."

"There's no reason to feel weird, Geordi. This is necessary information. Now, do I need to go over this with Toff?"

"No! No, thanks, I can show him how everything goes. In case he ever decides to have sex... you know, with someone."

Mom took the condom off her fingers, stuffed it back in the packet, and flicked a two-pointer right into the trash can. My eyes widened in astonishment. She crooked a smile at me. "Didn't know I played basketball in college, did you?"

"Mom, sometimes you amaze me."

"You amaze me too, Geordi. Let's cover one last thing on the subject of you and Toff and sex before we move on, my darling son. When it comes to any relationship, but especially a romantic one, always be honest, honey. With the other person as well as with yourself. Promise me you'll do that."

Dag. "Well… I'll try."

"Good." She reached over and took my hand again. "Geordi, are you having a problem with your dad?"

"Why do you ask?"

"Because I can sense some kind of tension between the two of you. I asked your father. He told me you got into a fight with someone over some pictures, but he didn't want to talk about what's going on with you and him, so I'm asking you now. If you don't want to talk about it either, that's fine—"

"I don't want to talk about it."

"Okay. I won't push you. But whatever it is, don't let it linger. No problem gets better when you just let it dangle there. And we don't always have as much time to fix things as we think. If you need to talk, about anything, I'm always here."

"I know."

She reached into her bag again and handed me a small tube of K-Y Jelly along with the box of condoms. Then she stood up, leaned over, and kissed me on the forehead. "Good night, honey."

"Good night, Mom."

I FELT clean and refreshed from my shower and was tucked comfortably in the bed farthest from the door because Toff said he wanted to sleep in the other one. The overhead light was off, and the small lamp on the nightstand between the two beds gave the room a soft, intimate glow. Tired and with the clock well past midnight, I turned on my side and drew my knees up in my favorite slumbering position. I lay that way for ten minutes, but sleep wouldn't come.

Maybe it was the hiss of the shower that kept me awake. Or the sound of Toff bumping around in the bathroom. I rolled onto my back and stuffed the extra pillow under my head. That didn't help either. I just stared up at the slowly circling blades of the white ceiling fan.

The shower shut off. More thumping and bumping followed. The blow dryer came on for a few minutes, its hum drifting soothingly through the semidarkness of the room. Then the door opened and Toff emerged naked from the bathroom. *Jeez. Ever heard of boundaries, man? At least I put my underwear back on after my shower.*

Toff eyed me as he walked across the room and stopped beside the other bed. His spiky hair was still a little damp, and his body gave off the pleasantly warm scent of shampoo and soap. "What's wrong, Geordi?" he asked.

"Nothing." *You're just making me fick-facking nervous with your junk hanging out all over the place.*

He sat down on the bed with his legs spread apart. I looked up at the ceiling fan again. "Your mom chewed you up for bringing me out here, didn't she?" he said.

"Yeah. She's gonna ground me or something when this is all over."

"Sorry. I didn't mean to get you in trouble."

"It's okay. I'm glad I could be there for you."

Toff rubbed his hands back and forth over his scalp several times, as if trying to tame his hair.

"Are you okay, man?"

"I don't know, Geordi." He let his hands flop down beside him. "I feel kinda crazy in the head. I just want to know. I just want to know what happened to my dad."

"You will. That sheriff will find him."

Toff got up and walked over to the minibar. Mom raided it before she left, taking all the liquor and leaving only two small bottles of cranberry juice. "You want some juice?" he asked over his shoulder.

"No, thanks."

With his back to me, he twisted off the cap and turned the bottle up, tipping his head back. I found myself looking at him again. God, my friend was hot. My friend was so *damn* hot.

After downing the juice, Toff dropped the empty bottle in the trash can. He squinted. "There's a used condom in here," he said in a what-the-hell tone.

"Oh. Uh… yeah. My mom was giving me instructions on how to use one. Did your dad ever teach you that?"

"My dad never taught me anything." He crossed the room and threw himself on the other bed. He folded his hands behind his head and stared up at the ceiling.

"Do you want to talk?" I asked.

"I thought we were already doing that."

"I mean do you want to talk about your dad."

"No." His voice was flat, but I could still hear the pain in it.

"Toff, I don't think you're doing yourself any good holding everything in about your dad."

"What am I supposed to say, Geordi? Huh?"

"Tell me how you feel about him."

"What good is that supposed to do? I feel angry that he was never there, *ever*, in fifteen years. I feel afraid for what might have happened to him. And I feel confused because I never understood him. I feel confused because I don't know if my dad ever really loved me. Telling you that doesn't make anything clearer in my head. It just makes me feel like I'm going out of my mind. So what good is talking about this?"

"It helps to remind you that you're not alone in this. I'm here. I'm listening. You've got somebody in your corner. And it helps me to understand you."

Toff paused for a few moments, as if letting what I'd said sink in. The angry scowl on his face softened. "Thanks, Geordi. Thanks for everything you've done for me. I don't know what I would've done if I didn't have you."

"You've got Jess too. And Jake."

"But they're not as close to me as you are." He turned on his side, facing me. "Is it okay if I come over there with you?"

Oh jeez. "Yeah."

He slid off his bed, walked over and lifted the covers off me. As he raised his knee to climb in, I held up a hand. "Wait, Toff. Can you… put on some underwear or something?"

He smiled as if I were making a joke. "Why?"

I thought about being honest with him. I thought about telling him the truth, that the idea of having his naked body next to me in bed was scary as hell.

"Never mind," I said, putting his comfort ahead of mine once again. "Just get in."

He reached over to turn off the lamp. Then he climbed in next to me and pulled the covers tight over us both.

We didn't talk after that. I don't know about Toff, but my mind went south once his chest and thigh were pressed against me. We lay together, motionless and silent, for what seemed a very long time, taking comfort in each other after one long monster of a day. But gradually something gloriously magical and intense blossomed out of that intimacy. Toff's body was firm, warm, his skin smooth, and the scent of the soap from his shower was intoxicating. I'd never slept in the same bed with another guy before, especially not a naked guy. My heart started pounding. Why was I so afraid?

Toff pressed closer to me, and I realized my heart wasn't pounding from fear. Heat rose through my body, and suddenly it felt good and right that Toff was the naked guy in bed with me. He had his arms around me, and I couldn't remember when that had happened. Toff kissed me, hard and greedily at first, then soft and tenderly. So much pain. He was in so much pain. I could feel it in every kiss, in every caress he gave me. *Toff. Oh Toff. I wish I could take your hurt away.*

There was more than pain in his touch, however. I could feel how much he loved me, how much he needed me. I reached for him with a passion I'd never felt before. No, wait; I *had* felt this passion, many times, I'd just never given in to it before. Toff slid his hand beneath the waistband and down the back of my shorts and grabbed on, and there was nothing horrible about that. Nothing at all. His body in my arms was like finding a part of me that had long been hidden away somewhere.

He got me out of my underwear, we rolled our bodies together between the sheets, and I discovered how much hotter it is to have another guy's hand on the rudder. So to speak.

WE SHOWERED again, together this time, washing the residue of fresh sweat off each other's bodies. Then we dried each other with thick, cottony towels bearing the logo of the bed and breakfast, and we climbed back in bed. Toff curled on his side, took my wrist, and pulled my arm protectively around him. I snuggled in close behind him. He closed his eyes, looking more relaxed than he had in days, and said something so softly that I didn't understand a word of it. But his message came through clearly anyway. I felt his gratitude and his affection in the placid, settling moves of his body.

In two minutes he was asleep.

I was glad he'd found some peace, though I couldn't be sure how long that would last. Something had changed for me too, something perhaps more lasting. I didn't try to puzzle out that something. It was very late, close to two in the morning, and I didn't have the energy to analyze my own feelings. I watched Toff sleep for a while, accepting the wonderful satisfaction of having this moment with him.

Then my satisfaction carried me gently down into slumber.

CHAPTER 15

FAR, FAR away, a phone rang. A jangly, annoying sound.

It rang for a long time.

Jeez. Stop already.

Something or someone moved, reached out. There was a click. "Hello?" The voice was husky with sleep. Toff's voice. "Okay… yes, we're up. Just give us ten minutes and we'll meet you there…. Okay, bye."

A clunk and a click as the receiver went down, and then an elbow nudged me in the side. "Hey. Geordi. Wake up."

"No." My voice sounded like gravel rolling over gravel.

"That was your mom. She says it's nine o'clock. She wants us to come to breakfast."

"'Nother time…." I reached over and tried to haul him back against me.

He laughed and pulled away. "No. Your mom said now." The bed bounced slightly as he rolled out. He walked around to my side, leaned over, and kissed me on the chin. "Come on, let's go." Then he swatted me on the butt. Hard.

"Owwy! Who died and made you boss? Dag."

While we were getting dressed, I paused for a moment to send a text to Jessica. I got back a response that went: *Jessica doesn't have cell phone privileges. Try her again in about 100 years.*

Eek.

"Is Jess okay?" Toff asked.

"Oh yeah. Sure. She's fine."

THE DINING room was cozy like the rest of the place. There were eight tables, enough to accommodate guests from every bedroom. Four of them were occupied with older white couples who chatted happily over their morning meals. Mom and Dad sat at a table on the north end of the room, beside a sunlit window with bright yellow curtains. Dad waved and smiled for us to come over. *Thanks, but no.* I waved and fake-smiled back and had the hostess seat Toff and me at a table on the south end of the room.

"Are you mad at your dad?" Toff asked.

"No," I replied, gluing my eyes to the menu.

"Geordi, don't hide stuff from me. What's wrong between you and your dad?"

"It'll work out, Toff. Don't worry."

The waitress, a slim middle-aged woman in jeans and a pink blouse, appeared before Toff could press further. "Good morning, guys. What can I get for you?"

"You know what you want, Toff?"

"I'll have a BLT on wheat with mayo and pickles and a glass of cranberry juice."

"All right, sir." As she jotted down Toff's order, the waitress turned to me. "And what about you?"

"I want the banana pancakes and a glass of milk, please. Oh, and that's my mom over there." I pointed. "Make sure she gets the check."

TOFF AND I had a good time talking possible plot points in the upcoming *Star Trek* sequel, which would be opening next Friday. We made no plans for making the opening together, however, since I didn't know if I'd be allowed out of the house then. We talked long after we'd finished breakfast, sipping on refills of milk and juice the waitress graciously provided. I could have sat with Toff that way for the rest of the morning, but then Dad got a call on his cell phone. After he finished the call, he spoke to Mom, and then he pulled money from his wallet and put it on the table to cover our meals. When they stood up, I could already feel a cloud of dread settling over my good mood.

They walked over to our table.

"Boys," Dad said, "the sheriff just called. She wants us to come to the station."

THE SHERIFF'S station was a short distance off Highway 64 on Route 24 about two miles outside Selmer. It was a sprawling, single-story building with a glass front on one end where the main entrance was located, tucked beneath two massive oak trees in the middle of an otherwise open field. Dad parked at the end of a row of four gray and black patrol cars. When he and Mom walked into the front office with Toff and me following, a uniformed deputy seated behind a wide counter looked up at us with a friendly smile. "Good morning," he said.

"Good morning," Dad returned. "We're the Quintrells. Sheriff Villanova asked us to come in."

"Oh yes. She told me to bring you right on back." The deputy stood up. "Her office is this way."

He led us down a hall to a frosted glass door. He rapped a knuckle on the door's metal frame. "Yes?" Sheriff Villanova's voice, though muffled, was as cool and commanding as it had been last night.

The deputy pushed the door open. "The Quintrells are here, ma'am."

The deputy held the door and ushered us into an office cluttered with metal file cabinets and shelves lined with books and copies of various penal codes. Sheriff Villanova was sitting behind a big metal desk, her eyes on the screen of a computer monitor. She was still wearing the same uniform she'd worn last night; I could tell by the small tear in the seam of her shirt over the left shoulder. The fact that she had just pulled an all-nighter didn't show on her at all. She gave us a restrained smile and said, "Good morning, thanks for coming in. Please have a seat. If you boys would sit here, next to the desk…."

She waited while Toff and I took the two chairs at the side of her desk and Mom and Dad sat down in chairs at the front. Toff kept moving his hands—patting on his knees, flexing his fingers, rubbing his palms over his thighs—while Sheriff Villanova went to one of the shelves behind her desk and pulled out a big manila folder.

She returned to her desk and said, "There are a couple of things I want to go over with you." She placed the folder on her desktop. "We took a suspect into custody at the forest preserve last night. I'd like for Sandor and Geordi to look at some photos to see if they can identify the man who attacked them. Sandor, you first."

The sheriff opened the manila folder and held it out to Toff. He peered inside the folder for maybe ten seconds before jabbing his finger at something. "That's him."

"Okay," said the sheriff, shifting the folder toward me. "Now you, Geordi."

In the folder was a large photo sheet bearing eight headshots of white, twenty-something guys. I spotted Blondie right off, the second photo from the left on the bottom row. "That's the guy," I said, pointing.

The sheriff nodded. She grabbed a pen and handed it to me. "I'd like you boys to initial the photo you selected."

As Toff and I took turns with the pen, Toff said, "Who is this guy? Did he do something to my dad?"

"His name is Charles Beck," Sheriff Villanova replied. "He ran off from his home in Knoxville three years ago when he was sixteen, and he's been homeless since. According to him, he's been living in the forest preserve for the past two weeks. He says that yesterday he stumbled on your father's abandoned car. That's where he found the shirt, the boots, the cell phone, the gun, and the wallet he had on him."

"He had my dad's wallet too?" Toff said.

"Yes. The wallet had a driver's license and two credit cards in the name Gerald Toffler."

"He robbed my dad!" Toff rose up to the edge of his seat, his expression agitated.

"We don't have any evidence of that, Sandor," the sheriff replied evenly. "For now we're holding him on assault charges regarding his encounter with you kids."

"So you're saying my dad just parked his car, walked away, and left everything behind?"

Sheriff Villanova didn't answer. She took the sheet with the photo we'd initialed, placed it back in the folder, and put the folder aside. She never looked away from Toff, but something in her eyes softened.

A tremor went up Toff's left arm. He looked afraid. "Where's my dad?"

"Did you find Mr. Toffler?" Mom asked.

"Sandor," the sheriff said quietly, "I need you to look at another picture. We think it might be your father."

Toff's whole face collapsed. "He's dead," he wailed in a low, shaky voice. "He's dead, isn't he?"

"We dragged the lake to find the gun. We also found a body."

"Oh my God," Dad gasped, putting his hand to his mouth.

Toff's back had gone rigid, arching tightly. I reached over and put my hand on his shoulder.

"The body is at the county morgue," the sheriff continued, speaking directly to Toff. "I can take you there if you want to do this in person. But the coroner has sent me photos that can be used for purposes of identification. It's up to—"

"Show me the pictures," Toff said.

The sheriff turned the computer monitor around to us. She used the mouse to open a file, and a slideshow appeared on the screen. The first shot was of the head, neck, and bare shoulders of a man lying on an examination table. His eyes were closed, his mouth slightly open, his dark hair draped in damp strands over his scalp, and his skin was a mottled gray. The facial features were distorted by bloating, but I still recognized the sad and lonely face of Mr. Toffler.

His mouth hanging open, Toff reached out with his hand as other images of his father began to slide across the screen, but he stopped short of touching the monitor. "Dad...."

"Sandor," the sheriff said gently, "I need you to confirm the identity. Tell me the name of the man in these photos."

"It's my dad," Toff answered without looking away from the pictures. "It's Gerald Toffler."

"Thank you. And I'm very sorry for your loss."

Toff kept staring at the pictures. He didn't cry or scream. His face remained blank, and that was somehow worse than if he had broken down. I reached over and put my arms around him. Mom and Dad came over and put their arms around us both.

"WHAT HAPPENED to him?" Mom asked. She was sitting on a sofa at the back of the office. Toff was lying with his head in her lap. He seemed dazed or shocked. "Did that Charles Beck murder him?"

"We have no evidence of that," said the sheriff. She had pulled a coffee maker off one of the shelves and placed it on her desk. As the coffee brewed, she set out three mugs. "I checked Mr. Toffler's last financial transactions. The Sunday he left home, he used a credit card to fill his gas tank, get an oil change, and replace two tires. Given that and the luggage he had packed in the trunk, it appears he was planning to take a long road trip. My theory is that he changed his mind and turned down the road to the forest preserve. When he reached the entrance, he got out of his car, left everything behind, and went through the woods to the lake. There were footprints in the mud at the edge of the lake that matched the sneakers he was wearing when we recovered his body, and those were the only prints in that area. We found him about thirty feet from shore, in ten feet of water. His body was weighed down by a pretty hefty rock. He had it tied to his waist by a short rope. It appears he walked out as far into the lake as he could, dropped the rock, and pushed it along the bottom until he couldn't get his head above water anymore. The coroner hasn't ruled on the cause of death yet, but my guess is that he committed suicide."

I was slumped in one of the chairs by the sheriff's desk, trying not to cry. Dad sat in the chair next to me, staying nearby. I was glad he was there.

Sheriff Villanova poured coffee in the mugs. "Where is Mrs. Toffler?" she asked.

"She died about thirteen years ago," said Dad.

"Then who is Sandor's next of kin?"

Dad exchanged looks with Mom and then with me before turning back to the sheriff. "He told us his father was the only living relative he knew of."

Sheriff Villanova frowned as she placed the carafe back on the coffee maker's heating plate. "I'll have to notify Children and Family Services about Sandor's situation. They'll have to make arrangements for his care."

"Do what you have to do, Sheriff," Mom said. "But Sandor can stay with us for the time being."

"I'll be sure to let the social worker know that." The sheriff picked up two of the mugs, handed one to Dad, and carried the other to Mom.

"Thank you," Mom said as she accepted the mug. She took a sip and then frowned. "Sheriff, doesn't this business about carrying a rock into the lake and drowning seem suspicious to you? Why would someone go to such lengths to commit suicide when he had a gun?"

"If you're implying that Mr. Toffler was murdered," the sheriff answered, "the same question applies. Why would the killer go to such lengths when he could have just used the gun? Suicidal people are usually distraught. Who knows what goes through a person's head when he decides to kill himself?"

Mom shrugged, seemingly conceding the point. "When will we know the official cause of death?"

"That depends on the coroner," said the sheriff. She went back to her desk, sat down, and picked up the third mug. "He's thorough, but he tries to wrap these things up as quickly as possible."

"But once the coroner has ruled, he'll release Mr. Toffler's body to the next of kin," said Dad.

"Yes, that's usually how it goes."

"What about Mr. Toffler's possessions?" Dad asked. "His car, luggage, wallet… when will those be released?"

"I'll have to hold those until the investigation is complete and Charles Beck has been tried. That could take several months. But I won't hold them any longer than I have to."

Mom looked down at Toff, who had closed his eyes. She stroked his forehead with her fingers. "Do you need anything else from us?"

"No, Mrs. Quintrell, I have everything I need for now."

"Then my husband and I are going to get these boys back home."

Walking out of the sheriff's office, I leaned against Dad, and he slid his arm around my shoulders.

JESS WAS sitting on our front porch when Dad turned the car into our driveway. She got to her feet as Dad shut off the engine and we climbed out of the car.

Mom and Dad gave Jess a quick greeting as they passed her and went into the house. Jess stood face-to-face with Toff and me. She kept studying Toff's face, trying to assess his feelings. Toff still looked the way he had in the sheriff's office, empty and emotionless, as if something in him had been shut down.

"Oh, Toff," she said as she threw her arms around his shoulders. "I'm so sorry."

"How did you know?" I asked her.

"The sheriff sent photos to a detective here in Memphis for me to do an ID on that guy we fought in the woods," Jess replied. "The detective told me about Mr. Toffler."

Jessica didn't seem as if she would ever let Toff go. I knew she was grounded. Either she'd skipped out on her punishment or Mrs. Sanchez had granted a temporary reprieve. More likely the latter. Either way, I wasn't surprised to see her. Toff closed his eyes as he rested his head against her shoulder and took in her comfort.

"I'm glad you're here, Jess," Toff whispered.

"Where else would I be?"

CHAPTER 16

I SAT on the bench at the little wooden picnic table in our backyard. The table was in the shade beneath a big Japanese maple tree, but there was no breeze and the afternoon sun was relentless, heating the air to a steamy ninety-seven degrees. I didn't care about the hot and humid conditions. Tears streamed down my face.

Toff was asleep in the guest bedroom. He hadn't cried once. I couldn't stop.

My back was to the house. I heard the door open behind me. Someone was approaching, footsteps swishing over the grass. I wiped my forearm across my face.

"Honey?" Mom sat down beside me and took my hand. She didn't say or do anything else for the moment.

"I don't understand." I wiped my face again. "I don't understand how Mr. Toffler could do this to Toff."

"I only talked to Mr. Toffler a few times over the years, but I do know he was a very haunted man."

"I don't care if he was haunted. You don't abandon your kid because you got trouble. You deal, you get over stuff."

"That's not always so easy. And we don't know everything he was struggling with."

"What's Toff supposed to do now? How's he supposed to live?"

"We'll get that worked out. Try not to worry." She squeezed my hand gently. "You've had a lot to deal with yourself the past few days. Do you want to tell me about it?"

I sniffed noisily and rubbed the back of my free hand over my runny nose. "I need a tissue."

"Let me bring you some." She started to get up.

"No. Don't go."

She settled next to me again and waited.

After a few moments, I said, "I've been getting mad at Toff a lot lately. Sometimes he wanted stuff from me that I didn't want to give, that kept me from stuff that I wanted."

"And you didn't tell him how you felt, did you?"

"I couldn't. I didn't want to hurt his feelings."

"So instead you hurt your own, and then you got angry at him for it. This is exactly what I was telling you earlier, honey, about being honest. It's okay to say no if that's how you feel. And the people in your life, the people who are important to you, deserve to know how you feel."

"Well, as you just said, that's not always so easy."

"But you complicate your life and your relationships when you're not open and honest."

I sighed and leaned against her shoulder. "Mom, is Dad home?"

"He went to the museum to check on a few things, and then he's going downtown. We got a call from Family Services about Toff. Your dad's going to meet with one of their social workers."

"Are they going to take Toff away?"

"No, honey. Not now. There's a lot that has to be worked out for him, but he'll be fine here with us while we get that done."

"And after everything's done, what happens to Toff then?"

Mom put her arm around me in a hug. "Son, I promise you, Toff is going to be fine. Just make sure that you be there for him, okay?"

"Okay."

LATER, IN my room, I lay across my bed and tried to sleep. But I was too tired and emotional for that. The tears came again.

I cried so much because I hurt for Toff, because I knew that if my dad died, it would destroy me. I cried because I was terrified at the idea that Toff would get taken away now and I'd lose him for good. Yeah, I was being selfish again, thinking about my feelings when I should have been thinking about the feelings of my friend—my boyfriend. But knowing how much I'd hurt over the death of my dad helped me to understand what Toff was going through. And my fear of losing Toff helped me to understand how much I loved him.

The sound of Dad's car in the driveway caught my attention. I sat up and wiped my face with my hands. In the few minutes it took for him to park, shut off the engine, and work his way inside, I'd managed to compose myself. As I walked along the hall, I peered into the guest room. Toff was still sleeping. Good. He needed the rest. He would have to muster a lot of strength for what was coming.

Mom and Dad were talking in the living room, their voices low enough that I couldn't make out distinct words and get a sense of their topic. I wasn't interested in eavesdropping anyway. When I entered the living room, they stopped talking immediately. Dad hadn't even shut the front door yet; he stood there holding the knob in his hand, with Mom standing in front of him. Both of them turned to me. I offered a little wave and went, "Hey, Dad."

"Hi, Geordi."

I walked right up to Dad and stopped, waiting. Dad shut the door, and then he waited too. A little smile turned up the corners of Mom's mouth. "I'll go get dinner started," she said as she headed for the kitchen.

"Let's sit down," Dad said, and he led me to the sofa where we both sat. "How're you feeling? Your mom told me you were pretty upset this afternoon."

"Yeah, but I'm better now." It was hard to look at him. "Did you talk to a social worker about Toff?"

"Yes. He's going to stop by tomorrow to talk with Toff, your mom, and me. Your mom and I have to go through a certification process so we can keep Toff here until Family Services finds him a foster or adoptive home."

"Uh… can't you and Mom adopt him?"

Dad laughed, a quick, amused sound. "Did you really just ask me that? Come on, Geordi. We adopt Toff and your boyfriend becomes your brother. Exactly how is that supposed to work?"

"Oh. Yeah. I guess it wouldn't work." The fear started swelling in my chest again. I took a deep breath, trying to force it down. "Where will Toff go? Who will he live with when he leaves here?"

"I don't know. But I'm sure the state has plenty of good people lined up who want to foster or adopt a kid. And Toff is a bright, likable boy. He'll find his way into a good home."

"What if it's a home in another city?"

"I see where you're going with this, son. If it comes to that, we'll work something out so you and Toff can see each other."

"Okay. Thanks." I took another breath. "Dad, the other day… what I said… I didn't mean it. I don't hate you."

"I know that, Geordi. And I didn't mean to cause you any trouble when I posted those pictures on Facebook. Who beat you up over that, by the way?"

"Carson."

"Why would Carson beat you up over some pictures?"

"Because in the very first one, where you're telling everybody to meet my new boyfriend, it looks like Carson and I are the boyfriends. At least that's what his dad thought. And his dad gave him a hard time, thinking Carson's gay."

"You've got to be kidding me."

I presented my still-battered face to him, framing it between my upraised hands. "Does this look like I'm kidding?"

"I'm sorry, Geordi. I didn't think the pictures would be taken that way. And I'm surprised Mr. Meyer would take that attitude with Carson. I've never known him to say or do anything to indicate he was so homophobic. He seemed very open-minded when I told him you're gay."

"Yeah, well, maybe Mr. Meyer's open mind slams shut when it comes to his son being homo."

"I'll have a talk with Mr. Meyer, get this whole thing cleared up for you."

"No, Dad. Don't." I looked squarely in his eyes. "Can I be honest?"

"Please."

"I'm sorry for saying that I hate you, and I'm sorry for hurting your feelings. But Dad, you've got to lighten up. I don't need you to run every single bit of my life. You jump the gun on things and make decisions for me, and it's driving me crazy."

"Geordi, this nation has come a long way. Despite how it's evolved over the years, the United States... and most of the world... is still a place where it can be very hard to be black and very hard to be gay. You're an intelligent, strong, capable boy, but you're starting out with society already having two strikes against you. I don't mean to make your life miserable, son. It's just that you're precious to me, and I don't want things to be difficult for you. I'm trying to cushion you from the blows, so to speak."

"But I'm not a little kid anymore. I don't need you. Well, I mean, I still need you for some things. I'll always need you for some things. But you have to let me make my own decisions and work out my own problems. How else am I supposed to grow up if I don't do that?"

Dad nodded. "You're right. I suppose I have been overbearing with you in some regards. I think it comes from the way I was brought up. My father thought it took toughness to make a boy become a man. He never showed affection to Ronnie or me, never helped us through any problems we faced, but he was quick to come down hard on us when we got out of line. When I fell in love with another boy—"

"Whoa! Back up, Dad. *You* had a thing for a guy?"

"Sure, Geordi. When I was fourteen, I went head over heels for a boy who lived down the street from me."

"Did he feel that way toward you?"

"Yes, he did. You might say we were a couple for nearly six months."

"Wow. Do you still know this guy? I mean, is he still around?"

"Yes."

I took a moment to catch my breath. "Do I know him?"

"Yes."

"Who…?"

"His name is Steve. Grevney."

"*Dr.* Grevney? *My* doctor? You had a thing with my doctor? Jeez. I knew you guys grew up together, but I didn't ever even think…. Does Mom know about this?"

"Yes, I mentioned it to her."

"And she's okay with that? Wait. Dr. Grevney… he's married. His wife is the receptionist at his office. How could he be married to a woman?"

"Come on, Geordi. That little boy romance was over twenty years ago. You know lots of teens have same-sex feelings, and for many of them, those feelings go away and never resurface. The point here is that I was confused by my attraction to Steve, and I couldn't go to my dad to talk about it. He wasn't the kind of man who'd accept that his son could be gay and stand by him. Hell, he probably would have knocked the crap out of me if I'd told him." Dad reached over and put his hand on my knee. "I didn't want that for you. I wanted you to be proud and confident in who you are. I wanted to be the kind of father who accepted and celebrated all of you. And I'm glad you told me how you feel. I will step back and let you have your life, but I will be here, in your background, if you need me." He patted my knee and held up his hands. "So. We're good now, you and me?"

I just looked at him for a moment, this man who was the same dad I had known all my life and yet was new to me in awesomely wonderful ways. Grinning, I threw myself at him and wrapped my arms around his shoulders. "Dad, we're great."

THE NEXT morning, a social worker arrived at our house. He sat down with Mom, Dad, and Toff, and after an hour of discussion and the signing of paperwork, the social worker left Mom and Dad with temporary custody of Toff. Later that day, the McNairy County Medical Examiner officially ruled Mr. Toffler's death a suicide. The sheriff, in response to Dad's questions, advised that she found no life insurance policy among Mr. Toffler's effects. She did, however, recover almost four thousand dollars from his car and wallet. She said the money wasn't relevant to her investigation and wired the cash to Dad on Toff's behalf.

"What do you want to do?" Dad asked.

"I want to bring my father home," Toff replied. "I want to bury him next to my mom. I think he'd want that."

So Dad used the money the sheriff wired to have Mr. Toffler's body brought back to Memphis. Four days later, there was a morning graveside service under the hot summer sun. Mrs. Sanchez, Jess, and Javier were there. So were Jake and his mom. A lot of our friends were there, and even Carson showed up. About twenty people from the construction company where Mr. Toffler had worked paid their respects. Mom and Dad were there.

And I was there, right beside Toff.

It was a short, simple, beautiful funeral. A few of the coworkers shed tears. I cried a little. Even Jess had to blink to clear her eyes. But not Toff.

I didn't know whether that was strength or something else.

When it was over, Mom and Dad escorted Toff back to our car. I hung back, trying to figure out what I was going to say to Toff once I got him alone. When I saw Carson hurrying across the cemetery on an intercept course, my heart started racing. Surely this idiot wasn't going to jump me in a freaking graveyard.

"Hey, Geordi," he said in an odd, sort of nervous tone. "Can I talk to you for a minute?"

I noticed Dad had hesitated several feet ahead, looking back at me, ready to step in. I waved him on, saying, "I'll be there in a bit."

When Mom, Dad, and Toff had moved out of earshot, Carson lowered his chin and said, "I'm sorry for knocking you around, Geordi."

He leaned closer, dismay rising in his eyes as he got a good look at my injured face. "Damn. I beat the crap out of you."

"Yeah, and that really made my day. Thanks, Carson."

He actually looked regretful. "I shouldn't have done that. And I never should have said all that homophobic stuff to you. What happened with my dad wasn't your fault."

"I know," I said, surprised that I wasn't at all angry. "If anything, it was your fault. You wouldn't have been in the shot at all if you hadn't bumped into me." *Hey. This whole honesty thing is really kind of cool.*

"Yeah, that's right."

"So does that mean I get to beat the crap out of you now?"

He stood up straight in his dark blue churchgoing suit, dropped his hands to his sides, and lifted his chin. "Okay, man. Do what you gotta do."

"Carson, I was *kidding.*" Although, honestly, there was a teeny tiny part of me that wanted to give him a shot right in that dimpled little chin of his.

"Oh." He shook himself, looking uncomfortable and just a bit relieved. "Anyway, I got new respect for gays, man. My dad's been such a hard-ass about this. I mean, you should hear some of the stuff he says to me. That I'm going to hell, I'm going to get AIDS, people won't respect me, I'll never be a real man, I'll never have children. And he won't stop. I've told him a hundred times I'm not gay, and he's still giving me shit."

"I'm sorry to hear that, Carson."

"You don't have to be sorry because my dad's an asshole, man. Hell with it. He'll just have to get over himself. I really admire you now. You know the crazy stuff some people say and feel about gays, but you're not afraid to stand up and be yourself. That's so cool, man." He smiled and held up his fist. I smiled back and bumped knuckles with him.

"Anyway, I gotta go," he said. "My mom drove me out here, and she says I'll have to walk home if I'm not at the car in five minutes. See ya around?"

"Sure, Carson."

God. The world was truly going to hell.

Was I actually starting to like Carson Meyer?

MOM AND Dad held the funeral repast at our house.

"They're coming to see you, actually," Mom told Toff on the drive home from the cemetery, "to offer their support and sympathy. Do you feel up to greeting guests? It's okay if you don't."

"No, it's okay, Mrs. Quintrell," Toff said. "I'm fine."

It was mostly adults who showed up. Toff sat on the sofa in the living room to receive everybody. He was still wearing the new black suit Dad had bought him for the funeral, all handsome and dignified with his hair slicked back. I sat in the chair across from him, staying close, ready to swoop in if things got to be too much for him. He did great, smiling politely, shaking hands, accepting hugs, offering thanks.

A tall, slender man in gray slacks and a short-sleeved dress shirt stepped up to Toff and stuck out his hand for a shake. "Hello. Your name's Sandor, is that right?"

"Yes, sir."

"I'm Hank Magnum. Your father worked for me for many years. He didn't talk much, but he was one of the most efficient and resourceful employees I ever hired. You look a lot like him. How're you holding up?"

"I'm good, sir."

"Is there anything you need?"

"No. I'm all taken care of."

The man pulled a bulging white envelope from his back pocket. "We took up a collection for you at the office," he said as he handed the envelope to Toff. "My card's in there too. If there is ever anything I can do for you, please don't hesitate to call."

"Thank you, Mr. Magnum. I appreciate that."

As Mr. Magnum moved off to the dining room, Jess appeared in her black cotton dress and sat down next to Toff. "Hi," she said to both of us.

"Hey," I said. It was odd seeing her in a dress. "Your mom let you out of your cage again, huh?"

"Just for the funeral. But I've only got four more days in prison, and then I'm a free woman." She patted Toff's shoulder. "You hungry, fella? Thirsty? Want me to get you something?"

"No, but thanks."

Jake ambled over and sat down next to Jess. "That chocolate peppermint cake in the kitchen is awesome."

Jess grinned at him. "Thanks. I made that."

Jake leaned forward and looked at Toff. "Hey, I gotta leave soon. My mom's only giving me two hours off the leash today."

"Oh, yours too, huh?" Jess quipped.

"Come out to the car, Toff," said Jake. "I got something for you."

The four of us walked out to Mrs. Butcher's car. Jake opened the back door and pulled out the portable file. "I thought I'd better give this back to you while I had the chance," he said, handing the file to Toff.

Toff tucked the file under his left arm. The envelope full of money Mr. Magnum had given him was still in his hand. "Thanks, Jake. Thanks for coming. It means a lot."

I heard the front door snap shut. Mrs. Butcher had just stepped out and was heading toward us. Jake gave Toff a hug. He hugged Jess and me. "See you guys."

Mrs. Butcher offered Toff more condolences and then drove off with Jake. Jess, Toff, and I went to the guest bedroom. Toff placed the file and the money on the dresser. Looking at him and Jess, my emotions started swirling again. I had to sit down on the edge of the bed.

Toff took off his jacket, and Jess hung it in the closet for him. We might have talked or maybe started a game online, but Mrs. Sanchez walked in. "Time to go, Jess."

Jess clearly didn't want to leave, but she didn't protest. She gave Toff's hand a squeeze.

"Toff, baby," Mrs. Sanchez said as she slipped an arm around his shoulders, "would you like to be a part of my family?"

Toff's eyes seemed to spark. "What?"

"You've been banging in and out of my house for years now. You've always been like another son to me. I talked it over with Javier and Jessica, and with Mr. and Mrs. Quintrell. Everyone thinks it would be a good thing. I just wanted to let you know. It's nothing you have to decide today. Take some time, think it over—"

"Yes," Toff said right away. "Yes, Mrs. Sanchez, I'd really like that."

"Oh, sweetie." Mrs. Sanchez hugged him tightly.

BY THREE o'clock, all the guests were gone. Mom and Dad were in the kitchen, cleaning up. Toff and I had exchanged our suits and ties for jeans, T-shirts, and kicks, and we were sitting on the floor of the guest bedroom with our backs against the bed. He had the portable file on his lap and was looking through the various documents inside.

"Toff?"

"Yeah, Geordi?"

"Tell me the truth. Are you okay? I'm kind of worried because you haven't cried or anything since you found out your dad was dead, and you shouldn't hold stuff in."

"I'm not holding anything in. It hurts that my dad is dead. It hurts that he didn't really love me the way he should have. But he was so sad, so lost, and I'm glad he's at peace now." The look he gave me was stoic. "Don't worry about me. I'm gonna be fine. I'll be okay as long as I'm with you."

I got it now, why Toff had no tears. He was right about his dad. Mr. Toffler had never let go of his grief after that train crashed into his car and took Mrs. Toffler. He essentially died years ago, along with his wife. And Toff had grieved so many times for his dad that he had no tears left to cry for him. Unlike his father, Toff was ready to let go of sorrow. He was ready to embrace life.

I decided to stop hovering and give him some space. As I was about to get up, he came across something in the file that made him freeze. I leaned toward him, trying not to stick my nose in the file. "What is it?" I asked.

He didn't answer. His expression was one of awe and disbelief. Slowly, he pulled out a thick sheaf of photographs. The one on top was a slightly faded eight by ten of a smiling, pretty young woman with unruly brown hair. Toff broke into a huge grin. I'd always thought he looked like his dad. But now I could see that he had the same wild hair and bright smile as the woman in the photo—his mom.

I watched him as he began looking through the photos. There was one of his mom and dad sitting side by side in a boat with their cheeks pressed together. Another photo showed his mom in a gold graduation gown and cap, holding a diploma. And another showed her holding a baby—Toff—in her arms, with Mr. Toffler beaming happily behind them. As Toff went through the photos, he looked so innocently happy, so full of wonder. It gladdened my heart, opened up my soul, and I knew. I knew what Jess and Mom had known, what I had hidden from myself or refused to see—what I'd been afraid to acknowledge. I knew why I'd been so emotional lately, caught up in coils of feeling I couldn't sort out or make sense of.

I was in love with Toff. I had been in love with him all along.

In that moment, everything became clear. For so long I'd been uncomfortable with myself, so uncomfortable that I could barely stand to look in a mirror sometimes or let other people really know me. On some subconscious level, I hadn't wanted to accept that Toff had become something more than a friend. He'd been phenomenal in the way he showed his deepest feelings for me, and I'd practically shut him out, afraid of my heart. I'd short-circuited my own life by not being completely honest with myself and the people I cared about. Now there was no more confusion for me, and there was no more hiding. I loved this boy so much it seemed my heart would burst from it. The intensity of that joy brought fresh tears to my eyes. If I didn't get out of that room now, I'd start crying and laughing and babbling all at the same time, and Toff would think I'd lost my mind.

Later I would tell him just how much he meant to me. Later I'd tell him how happy I was that he was in love with me too. I leaned over, kissed his cheek, and then I got up quickly and left him to discover the mom he'd never known.

EPILOGUE

JESSICA'S QUINCEAÑERA celebration was beautiful.

Mrs. Sanchez rented a hall at the Pink Palace and decorated it with blue and white balloons, blue and white ribbons, and lots of white flowers. She also hired a band and caterers. Jess's friends from the neighborhood were there, and relatives from all over were also in attendance. Mom and Dad came too, of course.

Jess looked stunning in her blue ball gown with a white stone necklace and matching earrings, her hair swept up in an elegant swirl. She entered the hall as the band played a rousing song, escorted by her tuxedoed father. I was surprised to see Mr. Sanchez, and I feared there would be fireworks very, very soon. They stopped at a small table on the edge of the dance floor. Mr. Sanchez picked up the sparkling tiara there and placed it on Jess's head, a declaration that she would forever be his princess. Then he led her onto the floor for the traditional father-daughter dance. When they finished the dance, Mr. Sanchez continued following tradition by passing Jess off to her chosen escort—Caitlin.

Smiling, shimmering in a white satin ball gown, Caitlin took Jess in her arms and they swung out on the dance floor. That's when I expected the fireworks to start, but Mr. Sanchez just smiled at Jess and Caitlin. I guess he realized Jess meant it when she told him he could either get with her program or go to hell. He bowed to Mrs. Sanchez and took her hand and they swung out on the dance floor too. Along with her parents, Jessica's court of honor was supposed to join them on the dance floor at this point.

The quinceañera's court of honor was usually made up of chosen friends paired-off into mixed-sex couples. Jess wanted her court to honor her relationship with Caitlin, and her friends were paired off in same-sex couples. Toff and I were together. Jake was paired up with Carson. Even Javier paired up with one of the guys who played on the football team with him. Straight guys dancing together, straight girls dancing together—it was great.

Just before dinner was served, Mom and Dad said their goodbyes to Jess, reminded me what time they wanted me to be home, and took off. They didn't get the house to themselves much, and they probably wanted to take advantage of my absence and… well, you get the idea. Wish I didn't.

The food looked and smelled fantastic. After everyone sat down and ate a sumptuous meal, Mr. and Mrs. Sanchez made a toast to their daughter. Then, per Jessica's request, Jake grabbed his guitar, joined the band, and sang Stevie Wonder's "Isn't She Lovely?" while Jess and Caitlin led off another round of dancing.

There was nothing better than having Toff in my arms, looking into his beautiful eyes as we moved together across the floor.

A lot had happened in the three weeks since Mr. Toffler's funeral. Jess and Jake pulled ten- and fourteen-day groundings, respectively, but my mom only grounded me for a week. Blondie—Charles Beck—pleaded guilty to aggravated assault, theft, and trespassing and was sentenced to eighteen months in prison. That spared Toff, Jess, and me from having to testify in court against him. Sheriff Villanova released Mr. Toffler's possessions, and Toff was now the not exactly proud soon-to-be owner of a 2005 Toyota Camry he couldn't drive. He was also the soon-to-be owner of the house he'd grown up in, a prime piece of real estate in one of the most desirable neighborhoods in the city. We discovered that Mr. Toffler left $756 in his checking account and $17,000 in his savings account. Since the man didn't leave a will, Mrs. Sanchez hired a lawyer to go to court and get the money in the bank accounts and the titles to the car and the house transferred to Toff.

Toff moved into the Sanchez house last week, and it was just a matter of waiting for the completion of all the legal hocus pocus (which was being handled by the same lawyer) to make his adoption legal. Or that was the plan, at least. Mrs. Sanchez suggested that Toff keep the car, since he would probably be driving in another year, but sell the house and use the money to pay for college. The idea of selling the house sounded good to Toff, but he said he wasn't sure yet if he wanted to do that. It turned out that Mr. Toffler did have a life insurance policy; Toff found it in the portable file. He was the only beneficiary on the $50,000 policy. Mrs. Sanchez had already filed a claim for Toff, and he had agreed with her that they would place the money in a trust until he turned twenty-one.

Jake and Carson had been hanging out a lot more with Jess, Caitlin, Toff, and me, and now the two of them had gotten to be good friends. Jake was still rocked with the desire to kiss another guy. Carson even tried to give Jake advice on how to ask a guy out. In part, Carson's hanging out with us was an act of sheer defiance. His dad had finally accepted that Carson wasn't gay, but he wasn't crazy about his son spending so much time with the neighborhood queer kids. "I'll drag him into the twenty-first century if it's the last thing I do," Carson declared.

Toff and I had been pretty much inseparable since the funeral. If it weren't for having to go to separate houses every night to sleep, we would have stayed with each other around the clock. Emotionally, we were closer now than we'd ever been. Even when he finally bedded down at the Sanchez house, we talked on the phone late into the night, until one or the other of us was relieved of our cell phone by a cranky parent and told to go to sleep.

As the party wound down inside, Jess, Caitlin, Jake, Carson, Toff, and I sat together on a retaining wall near the parking lot. The sun had set, and stars were beginning to dapple the dark blue of the gathering night sky.

"This has been a great party," Carson said.

"It's official," Jess proclaimed, taking Caitlin's hand. "I am a woman now, badass, bi, in love with Caitlin Eisner and ready to be married."

"Yes, you are, babe," Caitlin agreed, then leaned sideways to plant a kiss on Jess's lips.

"Better be careful, ladies," Carson said. "Grandpa over there looks like he isn't down with what you're doing."

A middle-aged man who'd walked out of the planetarium scowled at us as he unlocked the door to his sports car.

Toff draped an arm around my shoulders and gave me a wonderful squeeze. "You know what? As long as I've got this guy in my life, I really don't give a shit how many dirty looks people give me."

"That's the spirit," said Jake.

"So what do we have to do to get you a boyfriend, Jake?" Caitlin asked.

"I don't know if I'm ready for a boyfriend," he answered. "I just wanna, like, take a guy out for a test drive. You know, see if I like kissing a dude."

As the disapproving man in the sports car drove away, a gray sedan pulled into a parking slot in front of us.

"Speaking of dirty looks," Carson said, sitting up straight, "here comes my dad."

Mr. Meyers, tall and hefty, climbed slowly out of his sedan. He spotted us right off, and the expression he gave us was indeed pretty close to dirty.

Carson stuck an arm straight up in the air, repeatedly jabbing a finger down at himself and Jake. "Hey, Dad! Check it out! My first kiss!" He threw his other arm around Jake's neck, leaned over, and plastered his lips to Jake's mouth.

"*Hell*-o!" Caitlin howled.

I think my jaw fell in my lap.

To Jess's and Caitlin's applause, Carson broke away from the kiss with a loud, slurping smack. "Mmm boy!" Carson snapped. He hopped down off the wall and turned to face a very dazed Jake. "Dude, you're a good kisser, but I don't have to do that again." He turned to Jess and Caitlin. "Gotta go, ladies. Had a great time. Happy birthday, Jess, and happy kin zee era. Hope you like the gift." Finally he turned to Toff and me with a happy grin. "Later, fellas." Then he ran over to the sedan where Mr. Meyer stood looking as if his whole head were about to explode.

"I *like* that fella!" I said, pointing enthusiastically after Carson.

Jess looked at Jake. "So how was it, kissing a boy?" she asked.

Jake flashed a big smile. "It's definitely something I want to do again." Then, after a moment, some other thought hit him, and his eyes lit up. "Hey, dudes and dudettes, I'm a bi guy!"

TOFF AND I left the museum with Javier, who headed home to get ready for a date with his latest girlfriend—number three and counting. Jess was right about his hell-with-it driving. I spent most of the trip with a hand over my eyes and a prayer on my lips.

When we reached the house, Javier hopped out of his car and dashed inside. Toff and I stopped on the side porch. He reached in and turned off the overhead light. Then, holding hands, we kissed good night. The kiss was long and slow.

"You can come in, you know," he said in a low, teasing voice. "Javier will be taking off in a few minutes. We'll have the place to ourselves until Jess and her mom… Jess and *Mom*… get here."

"Believe me, baby, I want to come in, but my parents told me to be home by ten. It's almost that now." He stared back at me with that familiar longing, so like my own, in his eyes. I kissed him again.

He sighed. "You sure you don't want to come in?"

"I'm sure I gotta get home." As I kissed him yet again, I let go of his hands and put my arms around him. My hands went everywhere.

"Hey," Toff said, squinting at me. "Are you feeling my ass?"

"Oh *hell* yeah."

Toff laughed as the door jerked open. Javier stepped out and towered over us, having traded in his suit for jeans and a T-shirt. He looked annoyed. "Geordi, do you know where you live?"

"Yes," I answered slowly, drawing out the word.

"Then go there. You know how my mom is about long goodbyes at the door."

I wanted to linger a bit longer, but Javier stayed where he was to make sure I took my leave. I leaned in to kiss Toff one last time, and Javier stuck his hand between our mouths. I gamely plopped a big wet smooch on the back of his hand.

"Ew!" You'd have thought my lips were covered in pure acid the way Javier wiped his hand on the sleeve of my suit.

I planted a quick one on Toff's lips. "I'll call you when I get home, sexy stuff."

Toff winked at me. "I'm counting the seconds, buzzy bear."

Javier snarled. "Mary Mother of God, stab me in the ears!"

WHEN I got home, Mom and Dad were cuddled together on the sofa in the living room, watching some sappy movie, probably a romcom. The syrupy violin music on the soundtrack sliced across my brain like a scalpel the moment I stepped through the front door. Triple ugh! And they have the nerve to hate on the movies I like.

I dutifully and painfully stuck my head in the space above theirs. "Hey."

Dad didn't take his eyes off the TV screen or his arm off Mom's shoulders. "Geordi. How was the rest of the quinceañera?"

"It was great. Everybody had a blast-tastic time. And Jessica's officially a woman now."

"That's wonderful. How's Toff?"

"He's good. I just dropped him off at home. I'm gonna call him now."

"Don't stay on the phone too long, honey," Mom said.

"I won't. Good night."

In my room I closed my door and took off my suit. That was a relief. I'd been starting to feel I'd been wrapped up tight as King Tut. My feet ached a little from dancing in my dress shoes, but everything was good. In my boxers and T-shirt, I grabbed my phone, crossed the room, and threw myself on the bed.

I looked at the painting on my nightstand, the one Toff had given me just a few days ago, an eight-by-ten watercolor he'd done on canvas that Dad had framed for me. It was a portrait of Toff and yours truly, his arm around my waist, my arm around his shoulders, our cheeks pressed together, our smiles glowing happiness and love. Those smiles showed we'd struggled and searched and found ourselves in each other. That's what I thought as I speed-dialed Toff's number. The picture was our past. Our present. Our always.

Toff answered after the first ring. "God! I counted almost sixty seconds. What took you so long?"

You could've lit up every house in the nation with my grin.

GENE GANT graduated from the University of Memphis. He has worked with the poor as a counselor for the state of Tennessee and as a corporate writer. He lives on a country lane outside Memphis.

ALWAYS
LEAVING

GENE GANT

When Jason Barrett wakes up, he remembers only one thing: his name. Frightened and driven by paranoia, Jason keeps moving, going from town to town working odd jobs and making no friends. When he stumbles onto an emergency in New Hanover and saves a fellow teenage boy, it offers him the first connection he's felt in a while.

All Ravi Mittal learns about his knight-in-shining armor is his name. Jason. But New Hanover is a small town and it is easy to reconnect. To return Jason's kindness, Ravi wants to help solve the riddle of Jason's missing past. As they work through clues, Jason begins to feel settled. He finds a place he belongs with Ravi—maybe something more.

But Ravi's father's deep-seated prejudice against the African American teen threatens to tear Jason and Ravi apart... if the mystery chasing Jason doesn't do it first.

www.harmonyinkpress.com

At nineteen, college freshman Mace Danner works as an escort, hiring himself out to customers who want a submissive they can dominate. Having no carnal urges himself, the sexual side of his job leaves him cold, but he sees the pain inflicted on him by his clients as punishment for causing his brother's death when he was in high school. Pain is not enough, however, to wash away his guilt, and Mace starts binge drinking in an effort to escape his remorse.

The dorm's resident advisor, Dex Hammel, sees Mace spiraling out of control and strives to help him. Despite the mutual attraction between them, Mace is disturbed that he still feels no sexual desire for anyone. Even with Dex's support, Mace's self-destructive behavior escalates, leading to a situation that endangers his life.

www.harmonyinkpress.com

IN TIME I DREAM ABOUT YOU

Gene Gant

Gavin Goode, a promising high school athlete with good grades, forfeited his future when he joined a brutal street gang called the Cold Bloods. The gang's leader, Apache, discovered Gavin is gay and framed him for murder. Now in prison, Gavin faces rape and abuse on a daily basis as gang members there attempt to break him. When his father is critically injured and Gavin reaches his lowest point, a mysterious ally appears. Cato is much more than the guard he seems. He has come from the future, and he possesses the technology to undo everything that's gone wrong in Gavin's life.

But meddling in the timeline has dire consequences, and Gavin faces an impossible decision: sacrifice himself and his father, or let thousands of innocents die instead.

www.harmonyinkpress.com

Is opening your heart to the possibility of love worth the risk of more pain?

After bouncing around the foster system since being removed from his neglectful mother, fourteen-year-old Linus Lightman is reluctant to trust or bond with his latest foster family, the Nelsons. He's sure they'll reject him as soon as they find out he's gay. He finds a kindred spirit in Kevin Mapleton, and their friendship quickly evolves into romance. But then someone posts a video of Linus and Kevin having sex on the Internet, and experience has taught Linus that the scandal will cost him both the Nelsons' acceptance and Kevin's love.

www.harmonyinkpress.com